ANOTHER VISIT TO...

DOYLES
CASEBOOK

by

ANN BRADY

Copyright Written Work: © Ann Brady
Copyright Images: © Ann Brady

Publisher: Pen & Ink Designs

ISBN: 9780993112980

CONTENTS

3

Other Works by the Author

Fiction:

Dear Friends: Letters From Abroad – Historical Fiction
Doyle's Casebook – Edition 1 – Crime Fiction
Little Friends – Picture Books
      Woodland Adventures Series x 6 books
      Garden Adventures Series x 6 books
      Farmyard Adventures Series x 6 books
Little Friends Colouring Book

Dracula: The Untold Story – Mystery/Horror Fiction
  (co-written with Rex Greenwood, decd)

WHO IS TOMMY DOYLE

Tommy Doyle is an ex-Detective Inspector in his mid-forties. He lives alone in an old three-story, brownstone building, in a district of LA. Tommy joined the police force after leaving school, much the same as his father and grandfather had before him.

During his time in the force, he met, fell in love with, and married a sweet girl called Mary. Much to both their regrets, they never had children, and as such Mary found the loneliness and stress of being a policeman's wife unbearable. There were many nights when Tommy didn't come home with Mary not knowing if he was alive or not. Doyle mixing with an assortment of bad guys often frightened her so in time, she came to hate his job.

The final straw for Mary came when Doyle's partner, Pete Mackintosh, came close to being shot dead. Fortunately, Doyle had turned the corner at just the right moment, saving his partner from some mad nutter who thought it would be fun to shoot a cop. The incident created a strong bond of friendship between the two men, which still existed to this day.

But for Mary, it was the end; she couldn't take it anymore.

Telling Tommy, they had drifted apart she made him choose - her or his job. It was a hard decision for Tommy; but even so, Mary wasn't surprised when he actually chose the job. Fortunately, they parted amicably. Mary eventually married a grocer and lives somewhere upstate. They also have three children, so she is happy, and for Doyle, that is all that matters.

After Mary left, she would often ring him, checking up to see how he was doing. As time passed the calls slowly petered out. It had been nearly ten years now since they had seen or spoken to each other. If truth be known Tommy did occasionally Miss Mary. It had been nice to come home to a warm house and a cooked meal. 'Oh well,' he had thought, 'it's all water under the bridge.'

Having left the force over three years ago; disillusioned and disappointed, Tommy had become a PI - setting up Doyle's Investigations. He had been a police officer for close to twenty years but had been driven out. Like Tommy and his pal Mac, most of his fellow officers believed he had been set up, but they couldn't confirm that.

It had happened whilst Tommy was working undercover.

Six months into the job he had discovered someone was trying to involve him in a criminal setup. Following twelve months of being investigated Tommy had been hauled before a disciplinary committee. He'd only just managed to avoid being incriminated when a surprise witness had come forward and exonerated him. Still, the whole experience had left a very sour taste in his mouth.

Fortunately, both he and the other officers at the precinct knew a local con-man had been involved, although the guy had somehow managed to avoid capture. Perhaps he had been forewarned and had fled the state, leaving Doyle's fellow officers with suspicions that someone within the force was behind the whole affair. Unfortunately, it was something they couldn't prove or follow up on, as connections with those 'upstairs,' meant the guy was protected.

About four months after being cleared Doyle made the decision to retire, or maybe he'd resigned due to being let down by those upstairs? It all depended on your point of view. Being disillusioned, and with the lack of support from senior management, it seemed it wasn't what you knew, but more a question of who you knew. He also found he didn't like the politics of the modern police force.

'I know who you are,' thought Doyle as he walked away from the precinct. 'And one day, you will pay. One day, wherever you are, I will get revenge.' Not that Doyle was one to bear grudges, but he never forgot where a debt was owed; either by him or to him.

As it turned out leaving the police force worked out quite well for Tommy. He'd set up his office on the first floor of the old brownstone building he called home. He had used his savings to rent two ground-floor rooms, setting up a spare bedroom in one room alongside his office. Eighteen months later a relative had passed away, leaving him with a sizeable inheritance. It meant he didn't have to work if he chose not to. When the owner of the building also passed away the brownstone came up for sale so Tommy put an offer in and purchased it. Overnight, he went from tenant to landlord.

Using some of the inheritance he moved his office upstairs to the second floor, converting the top floor into an apartment for himself. There was enough room to have a large sitting room, kitchen, and two bedrooms with ensuite bathrooms. At first, the ground floor rooms were made into 2 apartments, which he rented out to reputable people. But, more often than not he left them empty. After all, he didn't need the money.

Being a PI can sometimes be dangerous, so after much consideration Doyle decided to adapt the building, making it more secure. Once the last tenants had left, he'd had a small brick extension built at the back of the brownstone. To ensure secrecy he had used the services of a builder from out of town. The extension contained a hidden staircase that ran from the top floor to the bottom. To complete the job, a secret door leading to the staircase in the extension was installed in a store cupboard in his office. By the time the staircase was finished anyone visiting would be unaware of the buildings' secret. The idea of this secret entrance/exit would give him an alternate escape route, should he ever need one? So far, he hadn't needed one, but you never knew what might happen.

With Doyle's office now being on the second floor, he decided to expand the size of it. He added a kitchen and a bathroom, with extra rooms for storage and a gym.

Eventually, he converted the two ground-floor apartments into office units, which he rented out. The idea being, that as offices usually closed around five pm, he would have the whole building to himself in the evenings. It proved to work out well for him.

Over the last three years, Tommy had enjoyed being a PI. He still had links to the police force through his good friend Mac who occasionally helped him out with some bits of information; all unbeknown to the new man in charge, one Lieutenant Johnstone. Mac knew Johnstone disliked Tommy, but still, it didn't stop him from helping his mate when necessary. Mind you he wasn't the only one, as his colleagues were not averse to Dropping the odd helpful bit of information when Tommy needed it; as long as the Lieutenant wasn't looking.

Regardless of missing working on the Police force, and being around the guys he'd known for so many years, Tommy had slowly built up quite a solid reputation within his local community.

His favourite place to eat and hang out was O'Malley's Bar & Diner. A middle-aged Irish couple ran the bar; Pat O'Malley and his wife Molly, who cooked the food. She made a 'mean' Stew & Dumplings, Tommy's favourite.

The fact Doyle was an ex-copper wasn't held against him, and it had probably helped, as his presence had made the community feel much safer knowing he lived close by.

The short stories in this book are part of the follow-up to Doyle's Casebook, Revisited. Once again delve into Tommy Doyle's Case Files to discover the type of crimes he investigated and how he resolved them.

Hopefully, we will get to read many more shortly.

A PLEASURE TO MEET YOU!

After Doyle had put the phone down the only noise spoiling the silence of the office was the sizzling of the Resolve tablet fizzing in the glass of water. Poor Tommy was feeling rather delicate this morning, having spent the previous evening on a pub crawl. Not that he had enjoyed it, as he had been out on a job, following a foot-loose husband. Or at least that's what the wife, who had hired Tommy, thought. The husband had begun staying out late and the wife was worried that he had, as she put it, got himself a 'floozy.'

Three nights later, after watching and following the man, Doyle had proved there was no other woman. Just a husband going through a mid-life crisis or may be feeling the pressure of his job.

Either way, Doyle had decided, the case was a waste of time, even though he had two more days on it. At least that's what the wife, when Doyle had rung her, had asked him to give it. Reluctantly he had agreed; as long as he got paid, he didn't care.

Although Doyle owned the whole building, he occasionally rented out the two ground-floor offices. Initially, he'd been a bit worried about strangers entering the building so had installed a small bell attached to the front door. Whenever anyone entered the building the bell sounded in his office, meaning he could check the TV attached to the security cameras to see who it was entering.

After a couple of months, Doyle discovered the dentists' clients were inclined to leave the front door open so, for his security, he had hidden sensor pads under the linoleum of the third and fourth steps of the staircase. This meant anyone mounting the stairs caused a wall light in his office to briefly flash; just as it had done two minutes ago.

Checking the security camera screen Tommy noticed a slender-looking woman climbing the stairs. Shortly afterward a knock at the door caused him to look up. Seeing her silhouette through the frosted glass he waited to see if she would enter. However, she remained outside, apparently waiting for an acknowledgment to her knock. There was another sharp rap, this time slightly louder.

The tablet had dissolved so picking the glass up,

Tommy drank the fizzy water, before yelling out, "Come in."

There was a moment's hesitation before the woman turned the handle. Slowly the door opened. She stopped inside the doorway. Spying Tommy sat at his desk, enquiring, "Mr. Doyle?"

Tommy nodded, encouraging her to enter by waving and pointing to the chair on the opposite side of his desk.

Stepping forward she looked at the chair, then slowly closing the door she advanced further into the office and sat down. Clearing her throat, the lady asked, "You are, Mr. Doyle, the Private Investigator, are you not."

Tommy looked at her. He guessed her to be about forty years old. She had natural blonde hair and was slim built. Smiling slightly, he acknowledged her statement, saying, "Yea; I'm Doyle, and you are?"

Removing her glove, she held out her hand. "Marcia, Marcia Dobson. Mrs. Marcia Dobson, Mr. Doyle. How do you do."

Slowly Tommy reached across the desk. Taking her hand he shook it, finding it to be small and warm. "What can I do for you, Mrs. Dobson," he asked.

Swallowing, Marcia took some moments to gather her thoughts, finally blurting out, "I would like you to find my sister. She appears to have gone missing, and I am afraid that something terrible may have happened to her."

Tommy was surprised by the suddenness of the outburst. Taking a moment to consider the lady's request, he finally said, "If she's missing then surely the Police are better placed at locating her. Have you been in touch with them yet, Mrs. Dobson?"

"Oh! Yes," cried Marcia. "But they say they cannot do anything. They say they have investigated and it seems my sister has run away. But I know this just isn't true," and she began to cry softly.

If there was one thing Tommy hated it was a woman crying. He hated it because it always left him feeling helpless; not knowing what to do, or how to cope with the torrent of emotion.

Sitting back in his chair, he waited for the torrent of tears to cease. "Now, please calm yourself, Mrs. Dobson. Let's have a drink, and once you've settled down, we can discuss the matter further. Would you like a coffee?"

The lady nodded her agreement to his suggestion.

Leaving his seat, he quickly went into the small kitchen next door. Putting the coffee pot on he waited, allowing the woman time to wipe her eyes and calm herself. Once he felt she was back to normal he poured two mugs of hot, steaming coffee and returned to sit in his seat. Placing the mugs down on the desk, he said, "Sorry, I have no cream and sugar."

Looking at him, Marcia picked up one of the mugs, smiled, and said, "That's okay."

For the next few minutes, the pair sat drinking their coffee in silence. Tommy needed the caffeine fix, whilst Marcia needed time to settle her nerves. Peace reigned for about ten minutes, the only sound being the ticking of the wall clock, which was ten minutes fast. An old habit of Tommy's from his days as a cop when he used to set his clock forward so as not to be late for duty.

Finally, Tommy drained the dregs of his mug and placed it down on the desk. Looking at Marcia, he said, "Okay, Mrs. Dobson. Tell me about your sister and why you think she's missing."

Following Tommy's lead, Marcia placed her mug on the desk. He noted she'd left a small amount of coffee in the bottom of the mug, and the marks of pink lipstick on the side where she had sipped the hot beverage. Taking a deep breath, she slowly began to tell him all she knew. As she did Tommy jotted notes down on the pad in front of him.

Marcia's sister was called Doreen Smith. 'An old-fashioned name,' thought Tommy as he wrote it down. She was nineteen years old and unmarried. The sisters had arrived in the city some four years ago; not long after their grandfather had passed away. He had brought them up after their parents had been killed in a car accident, ten years previously.

Everything had been okay at the start. Marcia had found a job and they had a nice little apartment in a quiet neighbourhood. Doreen finished her last two years at the local school, doing quite well. She had then managed to get a job in a department store selling perfume.

It was about thirteen months ago that things had started to go wrong.

Marcia had married not long after they arrived in the city but her husband had turned out to be a 'bad-un!' They had split up, divorcing quite quickly. She had been so tied up with her own problems that she had missed out on what was happening with Doreen.

However, she quickly learnt that her little sister was staying out late. She'd also started drinking and mixing with the wrong crowd. The sisters had ended up arguing a lot.

Finally, one night Doreen hadn't come home; she'd just disappeared. Her clothes were still in the wardrobe. And despite asking around, no one had heard anything from her since. Marcia had reported her missing to the police but that had come to nothing.

Doreen had now been gone for nearly two months and Marcia was frightened something really bad had happened to her. Finishing her story, Marcia sat back in the chair, waiting for Tommy to say something, she felt drained and exhausted.

After a long silence, he said, "And you have no idea who these people were that your sister was hanging out with?"

Marcia shook her head, before asking him, "Do you think you can help me find my sister, Mr. Doyle?"

Looking her straight in the eye, he answered, "I can't promise you anything, Mrs. Dobson but I will make some inquiries. My usual terms are $50 per day, plus expenses. I'll give you three, no four days. If I haven't discovered anything by that time then I'm afraid you'll have to leave it to the police; deal?"

Marcia stared back, and reluctantly replied, "I understand and I thank you, Mr. Doyle. I accept your terms. When will you begin?"

Tommy stood up. "The sooner the better. But, as I haven't eaten yet would you care to join me for lunch, Mrs. Dobson?"

Rising from the chair, Marcia smiled. "Thank you but no, I must get back to work. Here is my address and telephone number. I look forward to hearing from you shortly." And with that, she shook his hand, turned, and quickly left the room.

After she had gone Tommy sat down to think. Picking up the phone he dialled the number of the local precinct and asked for Lieutenant Mackintosh.

Ten seconds later, a familiar voice growled down the speaker. "Whoa there! Tommy lad, how you doing? Not seen you for a few days," the man's Scottish heritage still showing in his voice.

Laughing, Tommy replied, "Yea, sorry, Mac, I've been working. I'm not bad, how are you?"

"Fair to middling," replied Mac. "And what can I do for you."

"What makes you think I want something," announced Doyle, trying to sound hurt at the question.

"Because I know you," replied Mac.

"Okay, you got me," confessed Tommy laughingly. "How about a spot of lunch and perhaps a few answers about a missing girl?"

Mac thought for a moment. "Okay, usual place one o'clock. What's the name of the girl?"

Looking at his notes, Tommy said, "Doreen Smith; aged nineteen, been missing a couple of months."

Mac made a note and saying bye he hung up. As he put the phone down, Mac wondered how Doyle had come across the girl's name. Going into the main office he questioned one of the detectives about Doreen. The man handed him a file with what little information there was. Returning to his office he studied it before leaving to meet Tommy.

Tommy walked to O'Malley's, his local bar. He was sat waiting at a table near the window when Mac pulled up in his car.

"Afternoon boys," said a warm Irish voice. It was Molly O'Malley. "Usual for lunch?" she asked. Both said yes, and as she left, Mac passed the file over to Tommy who quickly scanned the contents, before passing it back.

Once their food and drink had been served, Mac asked, "Tell me, why the interest in this particular girl?"

Taking a swig of coffee, Tommy said, "Sister came to see me. From what she says it seems the youngster got in with the wrong crowd. She reported it to the precinct but obviously, there wasn't a lot for them to go on. I just wanted to see if there were any further developments."

Mac shook his head. "Sorry, Tommy. As you can see not much happening. Hell, we have so many kids going missing these days that we have to go with the cases that are the easiest to handle. I know, it's bad, but we're undermanned, so what can I do?"

Tommy shook his head sadly. He knew Mac was right but it was a damn shame that it was that way. "Okay, Mac," he responded. "I understand. Anyway, I'll ask around and see if I can pick something up. I've given her four days, after which I'll throw it back in your court."

"Right," said Mac. "But, if you need any info let me know. I'll do what I can."

"Thanks," Tommy replied. And, as they finished their lunch they talked of more personal stuff.

Later, saying goodbye Mac returned to the precinct, whilst Tommy went to visit Doreen's place of work. Perhaps some of her workmates might know more about her lifestyle, and who she had been seeing.

Doreen worked at one of the nicer department stores; uniforms, nice make-up, hair-do, and pleasant manners. Taking the elevator to the second floor he strolled over to the perfume counter, taking in his surroundings he noted the people. In the far corner, the security guard chatted to a young woman; a customer. Approaching the counter Tommy pretended to be browsing the products on offer.

"Hello sir, can I assist you with a purchase," asked a young woman's voice.

Turning to face her, Tommy saw a young woman aged about eighteen. She stood looking at him with a smile on her face. "I'm just looking but I wondered if Doreen was working. I don't see her. I told her the next time I was in I would look her up, and if buying she would get the sale. Is she around?" And Tommy smiled at the young girl.

A frown crossed the young girl's face; for a moment, her smile almost slipped. Then gathering herself together, she said, "I'm very sorry, Sir, but Doreen doesn't work here anymore. Perhaps I can help you instead?"

Pretending surprise at the news, Tommy said, "She's left? What a pity, she was very good at her job. Do you know where she's gone?"

The young girl shook her head. Carefully looking around, she whispered, "I can't say. We've been told not to mention her."

"Why," asked Tommy, also in a whisper. "It's a perfectly innocent question? Surely there can be nothing wrong in talking about a past colleague?"

"Can I help you, Sir," a mature voice asked from behind.

Tommy slowly turned. Seeing a sour-looking woman; he presumed she was the Supervisor. He smiled. "I don't think so, thank you. This young lady is more than capable of answering my inquiries about the perfume I need." Finding herself outsmarted the lady had no option but to move away.

Turning back to the assistant Tommy smiled, "Now, where were we. Ah yes, you were telling me about this perfume," and he picked up the closest bottle to hand.

Seeing the assistant doing her job the Supervisor finally left, leaving Tommy with the feeling that it might be better if he left the shop. Handing the young girl his business card, he said, "Give me a ring later and I'll buy you dinner. No strings, just a few questions about Doreen."

The girl quickly hid his card in her pocket, nodding her head in agreement to the meeting, whereupon Tommy spoke out loud. "Well, thank you for your assistance. I think I should ask my wife if that's the correct perfume. I wouldn't want to buy the wrong one, would I," and turning he headed for the lift.

As Doyle strolled towards the exit, he sensed the security guard dogging his footsteps. He pretended not to have noticed him. Arriving at the lift he waited. When the doors opened, he stepped inside, the guard following him. Doyle pressed the top floor button and, just as the doors started to close, he slipped through them, leaving the guard stuck in the lift on his way to the top floor. He left by the staircase, laughing to himself at the stupidity of the man. 'That'll teach him,' he thought.

Two hours later the office phone rang. Picking up the handset he drawled down the receiver, "Doyle Investigations."

A timid voice spoke softly, "Hello, Mr. Doyle this is Gail Carter. You know, from the department store. We spoke this afternoon about Doreen."

He was surprised, for if he was honest, he hadn't expected her to ring. "Hello, Gail, thanks for calling. Where would you like to meet? You choose, I want you to feel comfortable and safe."

Gail laughed lightly down the phone, "Oh, I'm sure I shall be quite safe with you, Mr. Doyle," and she mentioned a small restaurant up town that would suit them both. With the time agreed, he hung up smiling. Young women today could be too trusting.

At seven o'clock, Doyle walked into the small restaurant known as Monty's. It sold burgers and pizzas and was crowded with young people. Seeing Gail waving to him from a booth he ignored the waiter and went to join her. "How you doing Gail; err I can call you Gail, can't I," he asked.

Gail smiled, "Of course but what do I call you?"

Doyle looked at her, wondering if she was trying to flirt with him, "Doyle. Everyone calls me Doyle. Do you want a drink?"

The waiter arrived, and once they had placed their order, he asked, "Okay, so tell me about Doreen. Why aren't you allowed to talk about her? Tell me what you know, please?"

Gail took a sip from her drink before she began talking. It appeared that Doreen had already been working at the store when Gail joined the company. The pair had quickly become good friends; Doreen taking Gail under her wing and teaching her how to do the job.

Not long afterward they had started going out together. They both enjoyed the cinema, music and even going to museums. The latter surprised Doyle, as he hadn't expected Doreen to be intellectual.

About four months ago, Doreen had started cancelling their excursions. She stopped going to the museums and the cinema but still seemed ready for a night out on the town.

Apart from at work, the two girls had slowly seen less and less of each other. Gail had been upset by Doreen's desertion, until one day she had finally faced her friend, asking her what she had done wrong. Doreen had laughed, saying nothing other than she now had other fish to fry and was in fact seeing someone special.

At first, Doreen had not wanted to talk about this other person, but two days before she disappeared, Gail had found her in the ladies' powder room in tears. Finally, she had managed to discover what was wrong. The man Doreen was seeing was married and she thought she might be pregnant.

"Do you know who this guy was," asked Doyle?

"No, not really, answered Gail, "Although, later that day I caught Doreen whispering with Mr. Stevens. They quickly pulled apart as I approached. Doreen looked upset. She walked away in a hurry, wiping her eyes. When I questioned her later, she denied that anything was wrong. That was the last time I saw her."

Doyle sighed; it didn't sound good news for the sister. "This Mr. Stevens - who is he?"

Gail looked up in surprise that he hadn't recognised the name. "His father owns the department store."

"Is he married?"

Gail nodded her head, and then suddenly cottoning onto what she had just said, asked, "Could Mr. Stevens have been Doreen's secret friend?" Doyle looked at her surprised face, agreeing that he may well have been.

Finishing their meal, the two-parted company. Doyle putting Gail in a taxi and giving her the money for the fare, which she at first refused, saying she could catch the bus. But he insisted, telling her he wanted to make sure she got home safely. After the car had pulled away, he lit a cigarette and began walking home. He needed time to think over what he had discovered. But, more importantly, he needed to decide what he was going to tell the sister.

* * * *

The following morning Tommy was in his office. A knock on the door heralded the arrival of Mac, two polystyrene cups of steaming hot coffee in his hand.

"Morning, Tommy," said Mac. "Thought you might need this," and he placed a cup on the desk. The steam circled up, the smell of the fresh brew hitting Doyle's senses.

"Thanks, Mac," said Tommy. "Smells great; just what I need." And taking a sip of the hot brew, he continued, "So, to what do I owe this early morning visit."

Mac swallowed a couple of mouthfuls of coffee, before replying. "Bad news I'm afraid, Tommy. We found a young woman's body this morning."

Doyle's head shot up. "My girl?"

Mac nodded his head, replying, "We think so."

"Oh hell," said Doyle, "How, when?"

Mac filled him in with the relevant details. The young woman had been found hidden in a garbage dump near a deserted building. The cause of death was, as yet unknown, and she was in a mess; blood everywhere.

Mac looked straight at Tommy, asking, "I wondered if you would come down to the morgue with me. The sister is coming in later this morning; she might need a friendly shoulder to lean on."

Tommy felt sick to his stomach. What a waste but he readily agreed.

Two hours later, Mrs. Dobson entering the morgue spotted Tommy. Heading straight towards him, she said, "It's a mistake, Mr. Doyle, right? It can't be Doreen. She can't be dead."

Tommy was stunned. He hated times like this. In all his twenty-five years as a cop, he had never got used to dealing with grieving relatives. Mac was even worse.

Mrs. Dobson was shaking. She was nervous, dreading what she was about to see. He gently took her arm and led her into the visitor's side of the morgue. As they entered, they were met by Mac who nodded at Tommy, before greeting Marcia and uttering the usual platitudes of sorrow at her loss.

Once they were ready the curtain was drawn back from the window and the sheet covering the body was carefully removed from the face of the victim.

Marcia stood, shocked at what she saw, before firmly declaring, "But… that's not, Doreen."

Mac and Tommy looked at each other. Mac asked, "Are you sure, Mrs. Dobson. The young lady matches the description of your sister."

Marcia turned towards him and, in a voice of authority, said, "Whoever that person is, she is not my sister. For a start, she has dark blonde hair; my sister's hair is a lot lighter. No… she is definitely not my sister."

After the curtain closed, Tommy led Marcia from the room, Mac following behind. Once in the corridor, Mac turned to Marcia, apologising, "I am so sorry. We honestly thought it was Doreen."

"I can see that the resemblance is close but no, I can assure you, it is not my sister," she replied, feeling a lot calmer now.

Mac nodding his head asked her, "Do you think we could have a DNA sample from yourself? Just to make sure, Mrs. Dobson."

Marcia looked at him in doubt; to her, there was no mistake but she readily agreed to his request, and the Police Doctor was sent for to take the appropriate sample.

After Marcia had left, Tommy joined Mac in his office. "The thing is Tommy, she looks like Doreen, and she did have Doreen's credit card in her purse."

"What," exclaimed Tommy. "Hell, no wonder you thought it was her. Oh well, we'll have to wait until the test comes back. I suppose in the meantime I should continue looking."

Mac agreed, asking his pal what he had found out so far, which Doyle was quite willing to share with him.

Mac 'hummed' at the news of the boss's son as that bit of news was something his guys hadn't come up with. 'Damn,' he thought, 'I wish Tommy was still on the job.'

An hour later Tommy returned to his office, thinking over what his next move should be. As he entered the building a voice stopped him in his tracks. "Mr. Doyle?" It was Marcia Dobson, "May I come in?" she asked.

"Of course, Mrs. Dobson."

The pair went up the stairs to the office, where he made them both coffees. Sitting opposite each other at the desk, he waited for her to explain the reason for the visit.

Eventually, having sat in silence for some time, he asked, "Was there something specific you wished to discuss with me, Mrs. Dobson?"

Looking at him Marcia took a deep breath before declaring, "That person wasn't Doreen. I would know my sister anywhere, and it wasn't her. Have you found anything out yet, Mr. Doyle?"

Wondering how she was going to take the news, Tommy was thinking how to tell her what he had found out, when she said, "You have found something out, haven't you. I can tell by your face. But perhaps it's something you don't think I'll like hearing?"

Tommy smiled, realising how astute she was, and throwing caution to the wind he explained about Mr. Stevens. He told her how he was married and there was a possibility that Doreen might have been pregnant, which could explain why she'd disappeared.

Marcia said nothing. She just sat absorbing the news. Finally, she replied, "So, if that person isn't Doreen, do you think this Mr. Stevens will tell you where she is?"

He shrugged his shoulders. Tommy was not sure that Stevens would tell him anything but he knew he would have to go and face the man.

It wasn't long after Mrs. Dobson left the office that he began to work out how to get to Stevens and the information he needed. But first, another coffee was called for.

Whilst Tommy was in the kitchen the phone began ringing in the office. Quickly grabbing a towel, he ran into the office to pick it up. "Doyle Investigations," he said into the receiver.

"Mr. Doyle," a refined voice asked. Doyle grunted yes, waiting for the caller to introduce himself.

The voice continued, "I understand that you have been enquiring about Miss. Doreen Smith." There was a short pause but before Doyle could respond the voice continued, "There is no point in denying it as I have it on good authority that you have been asking lots of questions. What do you want with Miss Smith?"

Doyle thought quickly. The only person who knew about his inquiries, other than Mrs. Dobson was Gail Carter. He responded with, "And why should that be of interest to you, Mr. Stevens?"

There was a short, sharp, intake of breath before the person on the phone said, "Well guessed, Mr. Doyle. So, tell me, why have you been asking about Miss Smith?"

Doyle, smiled to himself, replying, "And why should that interest you, Mr. Stevens; a married man."

He could hear the annoyance in Steven's voice. "Let's not mess each other about, Mr. Doyle; just answer the question. What do you want with Doreen?"

Doyle was tempted, just for a moment, to carry on annoying the man but realised, if he wanted information, he might do better to see how much he could learn from him. Finally, he said, "Well, Mr. Steven's, not that it concerns you, but Miss Smith's sister has become most concerned about her. She hasn't been home for two months. Her sister has reported her missing to the police. I am working closely with them to find the young lady. Can you assist us?"

There was no response only silence before Steven's shouted, "What do you mean the police are involved. She's not missing. Doreen is perfectly safe?"

Doyle was taken aback, as he had expected the man to deny all knowledge of Doreen's whereabouts, so he asked, "Well if she's as safe as you say, then why hasn't she been in contact with her sister. Surely she realises the worry and concern that her sister has for her."

"Well," responded Stevens hesitantly. "Well, it's not that I know exactly where she is, but she must be safe. She told me she was going away to think and would be back shortly."

"So," responded Doyle sternly, "you don't know where the future mother of your child is then? Anything could have happened to her, and you don't care. What sort of man are you to take advantage of a young girl?"

"What," yelled Stevens. "What the hell are you talking about? She's not pregnant. She just decided she wanted a break. She knows I would never leave my wife. It was all a bit of fun. She knew that."

Doyle couldn't believe the audacity of the man. Taking a deep breath, he said, "So, you don't know where she might have gone then? In that case, we have nothing further to say to each other, Mr. Stevens. I only hope for your sake that your wife doesn't find out what type of man you are. Good-day," and he slammed the receiver down, swearing loudly.

* * * *

The following day Doyle received an unannounced visitor; Mr. Stevens. The man was approximately six-foot-tall, aged about thirty-five, and reasonably good looking; which might explain why Doreen had fallen for him. He stomped into the office as if he owned the place. Looking around,

Stevens took in everything about the room, before saying, "Doyle, I presume?"

Doyle, in turn, looked Stevens up and down, deciding he did not like the man, so responded with, "Stevens, I gather? What can I do for you?"

Sitting in the chair opposite, Stevens started, "I want to get things straight about Doreen. Look, she knew I was married, and that whatever happened between us, would go no further. I love my wife. She understands perfectly what I am like. Doreen and I had a fling for about a month and then we both went our separate ways. As regards her being pregnant it can't be mine, even if I wanted it to be. I want you to back off, and stop pestering my staff?"

Doyle had listened quietly while Stevens had rambled on. Once he stopped talking, he let Stevens stew for a moment before responding. "And so, you deny any knowledge of where Doreen is, or why she is missing?"

Stevens looked at Doyle, a nasty expression on his face. "Yes. And if Doreen is expecting then it isn't mine. I can't have children; that's why it works well for me and the wife. So, whoever the father is, it most certainly isn't me."

His answer shocked Doyle. It was the last thing he had expected to hear. If Doreen was pregnant, then

37

who the hell was the father? Menacingly leaning across the desk, he said, "If what you say is true then what can you tell me about Doreen. I need to know it all and, as I am working with the Police, if necessary, I will come back to the store to talk to Doreen's friends. So, you'd better start talking."

After staring at Doyle, Stevens realised it would be in his own interest to tell all he knew. He wanted to make sure that no suspicion fell on him, especially if the girl had indeed gone missing. What if something bad had happened to her? Finally, he began telling Doyle how Doreen and he had met; and how their relationship had started, and ended.

An hour later, Doyle was alone.

Stevens had left annoyed. Even after confessing all he knew, which turned out to be very little in Doyle's opinion, the man had wanted his name kept out of any investigations. Tommy had taken great delight in telling him that he couldn't make any such promises, as he had no control over the police or their inquiries. Stevens had left dissatisfied.

Deciding he had had enough for the day, Tommy locked up and retired upstairs to his apartment. Perhaps a shower and something to eat would help him decide on his next move. If he were honest, at the moment he couldn't see any way forward; the girl had disappeared but where the hell had she gone?

* * * *

The following day, Tommy woke feeling a bit more positive about Doreen. He still had two days left to search for her.

First job this morning, after calling at his usual cafe for breakfast, was to go back and speak to Gail. He would also ask a few questions from the other members of staff who worked with her. And, if Stevens didn't like it, then the man would find out just how nasty he could be.

An hour later, Tommy sauntered into the perfume department and headed straight for the counter. Gail was surprised to see him. She checked the area to see if the supervisor was hanging around.

Tommy got straight to the point. "You mentioned something about Doreen enjoying going out; were there any places she particularly liked going to? This is important, so I need your help, please."

Gail seemed stunned by his straight-talking, and in a timid, shaky voice she finally answered him, "I'm not sure, Mr. Stevens would like me talking to you Mr. Doyle."

He swore under his breath then leaning over the counter, he harshly responded, "I don't give a toss what Mr. Stevens likes, or dislikes. I want some answers, and I'm jolly well going to get some. Or, I'll cause Mr. Stevens more trouble than he can handle. Now answer me, Gail, I haven't got time to waste. Doreen's life could well be in danger."

Shocked by his reaction, the girl began shaking. "Well, she liked going to Breezy's Bar. I didn't like it; it seemed so sleazy, and not the kind of place for me. I went with her a couple of times but stopped going after she changed."

Doyle stopped and thought for a moment, before asking, "In what way did she change?"

Gail swallowed, then replied, "She sort of became distant. She wasn't bothered whether I went out with her not. I think that was when she started seeing someone. But, I don't know who it was as she never told me. Does that help, Mr. Doyle?"

He nodded his head in agreement wondering who else, besides Stevens, Doreen had been seeing. As he started to turn away, he suddenly stopped; twirling around he asked, "Gail, by any chance do you have a photo of Doreen? The one her sister gave me is quite old."

The girl thought for a moment. About to say no she suddenly remembered. "As it happens, I do. We had one taken at a friend's birthday party not long after I started working here. Hang on, I'll go get it from my handbag." And with that she disappeared into a small room behind the counter, returning shortly with a photograph which she handed to him.

"Thanks," said Tommy. Turning he left the department as quickly as he could.

Just as he was passing through the ground floor of the store, a voice hailed him. "And what are you doing here again, Mr. Doyle?"

It was Stevens.

Doyle stopped, thinking that there was one man he could willingly smack. However, controlling his emotions he turned and looking at Stevens, he nastily responded, "Trying to find your missing employee, Stevens. Unless of course, you don't want her found, in which case, perhaps it would be better if the police were here instead of me?"

Stevens turned white at Tommy's response but before he could say anything, Tommy had left the building. He did not like the PI but had to admit he was right. Until Doreen was found, suspicion would fall on him, and that was the last thing he needed at this moment in time; his wife would not understand that. There would be publicity. If there was, then she really would decide to divorce him. He might not like Doyle, but he had better co-operate with him, for now at least.

'One day, Doyle,' Stevens thought. 'One day you'll pay.'

If Doyle had known the thoughts going around Stevens' mind, he would probably have followed his first inclination to smack the man. Fortunately, for both of them, he was ignorant.

An hour later Tommy was stood outside Breezy's Bar waiting for Mac to arrive. This was one joint you never went into alone. He would feel more secure with Mac at his back. Not long afterward his mate pulled up in his unmarked police car.

Strolling over he asked, "Okay, so how are we going to do this?"

"I thought I'd ask the questions if you'll back me up," said Tommy. "Better not announce you're a cop for the moment, let's see what happens. What do you think?" Mac agreed.

Entering the bar, they noted that at this time of day the place was deserted. Getting the barman's attention, Tommy pulled out the photo of Doreen.

"Have you seen this girl in here? Might be a few weeks ago but she was probably a regular."

The man hardly glanced at the photo, shaking his head no. His action annoyed Tommy so he grabbed the man's shirt, and in a menacing voice, said, "Now this time look at the photo, and answer the damn question. If anything has happened to her, and you know about her but didn't speak, then my friend here will make sure you go down for her murder, do you understand me?"

The man turned white as Mac quickly flashed his badge at him.

"Okay, okay," he said. "Let me look at the photo again."

And this time, taking the picture from Tommy, he held it under the nearest light. "Yes, yes," he said, "I think I do recognise her. Reen, Coleen, no… Doreen, yes Doreen. Bit of a party girl. She was in here about three days ago."

His response caused both Mac and Doyle's ears to prick up. Mac asked, "How many days ago did you say?"

The guy thought for a moment before answering, "Three or maybe four. It was… err… Wednesday night. Yes, Wednesday."

Doyle chipped in, "Was she with anyone?"

The man thought again and then said. "She was with this old geezer. Posh-looking guy; aged about sixty, a real sugar daddy type. Doreen was all over him. They were laughing like kids."

"Has he been here before?" asked Mac. The guy shook his head. "No… never seen him before."

"Thanks," said Doyle, throwing a couple of bucks on the counter. "Come on, Mac there's nothing more to learn," and he started to turn away when another thought hit him.

Looking at the barman he asked, "Do you have CCTV in here?"

The barman, a bit nervous, automatically looked towards the hidden camera.

Mac leant over saying, "Let's take a look at the tape for that night - please."

Reluctantly the barman bent down and lifting a tape he placed it in the player. Fast-forwarding it to the appropriate section he showed who Doreen had been with. Doyle had the man stop the tape at that point. Looking at the image on the screen he suddenly realised who the old man looked like, thinking, 'It can't be.' But the more he stared at the screen, the more he knew who it was.

Mac realised that his mate had somehow recognised the man, "You know who it is, Tommy?"

Doyle nodded his head, before saying, "I'm not sure. I need to go and see someone. Will you give me a couple of hours?"

Mac readily agreed. He knew how Tommy worked, and if anyone could solve the mystery then he could. He also knew that Tommy would give credit to the force if he could.

The two men parted company outside the bar; Mac returning to the precinct, Doyle to arrange a special meeting.

Two hours and a few phone calls later, a large black car pulled up outside the brownstone building. The front door opened. Two people entered and mounted the stairs, causing the light to flash in Doyle's office. He prepared himself for the meeting.

A knock at the door announced the arrival of the visitors. Tommy yelled out, "Come in," then he sat back down and waited.

As the door opened a young woman enquired, "Mr. Doyle. I believe you are expecting us?"

Standing, Tommy watched with interest as a young woman entered the office. She was wearing a well-tailored outfit topped with a three-quarter length mink coat. There was a small delicate hat with a flimsy net veil perched on top of her well-coiffured hair. On her feet were small heeled shoes, and she carried a matching leather handbag. To say Tommy was surprised would be an understatement; he was in fact, gob-smacked.

The young woman walked forward, her hand held out in greeting which Tommy took in his own to shake, "How do you do, Mr. Doyle. I understand you have been looking for me?"

Tommy nodded his head, before looking at the gentleman standing behind the woman. He matched the image on the bar TV screen exactly and as he came forward, hand extended, Tommy said, "Mr. Stevens, Senior, I presume?"

The man smiled, which surprised Tommy as he had expected an older, more severe copy of the younger Stevens.

"How do you do, Mr. Doyle. I am told I, or should I say we, owe you an apology for putting you to so much trouble," and the pair sat in the chairs on the opposite side of the desk.

Sitting down, Tommy looked at the pair questioningly, before saying, "Miss. Doreen Smith?"

The young woman coughed to clear her throat, "Yes. Or at least I was. I am now Mrs. Ronald Philip Stevens, the Third," and she smiled warmly as she looked at her husband. Continuing, Doreen looked back at Tommy, "I am so sorry for the problems I have caused you, but if I explain then maybe you will understand?"

Despite himself, Tommy found himself smiling in return, "I believe it is your sister to whom you should apologise, not me. Do you realise the amount of worry and concern that she has gone through over the last few months?"

"But, I sent her a letter. I told her I was going away but that I would be back in a couple of months. I wrote there was nothing for her to worry about," cried Doreen. "Did she not get the letter."

"Apparently… not," responded Tommy, causing the young woman to look at her husband, distressed by the news.

"What could have gone wrong," she asked Stevens Senior. "The letter did get posted, didn't it, Ronald?" Her husband confirmed that the letter had indeed been posted so he could not, therefore, offer any explanation for it going missing.

"Perhaps, if you could explain what has happened. The police will need to know that you are alive and, of course, your sister needs to be reassured that you are safe," explained Tommy.

Shocked at the news that she had been reported missing, Doreen took a deep breath and began explaining everything that had happened over the last few months.

It seemed that having had a slight fling with the younger Stevens, he had quickly become bored and had thrown her over. This had caused Doreen to become quite upset. She had been crying when his father had come across her. He had managed to get her to explain why she was upset, becoming quite annoyed at the behaviour of his son.

To make amends for his sons' bad behaviour he had taken Doreen under his wing, convincing her to have dinner with him. Their friendship, or should it be said romance, had blossomed from that moment onwards.

The fun-loving Doreen had only been a fling for the son. She had quickly discovered that it was her love of music, the theatre, museums, and everything associated with the arts that appealed to the father. Ronald, without realising it, had fallen in love with Doreen.

And she, finding a man who cared for her, had likewise fallen in love with him. Yes, it had been a quick relationship but they soon realised that they had been seeing each other nearly every day for close to six months.

Then about two months ago Ronald had taken the plunge, asking Doreen to marry him. She had been delighted, immediately saying yes. But Ronald had wanted her to be doubly sure, due to their age difference. They had agreed to go away for two months to see if they could live together. Those two months had been the happiest she had had for the last year. Finally, they agreed that marriage would not be a problem for them; for others maybe, but not them. They had gone abroad to be married.

Although Tommy was surprised, he still questioned, "But, you were in Breezy's Bar last week; why?"

Ronald said, "Perhaps I can answer that one, Mr. Doyle. You see, I wanted Doreen to be sure she wouldn't miss that kind of life, so we agreed to go there together. We had fun that night but to be honest it's not the kind of place we will be visiting again."

"Well," responded Tommy, "I am very happy for you. Just one other thing. Gail told me she thought you were pregnant?"

Smiling, Doreen responded, "Well, to be honest, I did think I was. It was after I told Ronald Junior that I realised I couldn't be which was when he threw me over. He was quite cold; seeming to take great delight in telling me he couldn't be the father and calling me a rather unpleasant name. That is why I was so distressed when Gail came across me."

Tommy nodded his head, before saying, "I understand. My apologies Mr. Stevens, but your son is not the nicest of people."

Mr. Stevens replied, "I agree with you, Mr. Doyle. His Mother spoiled him too much and I was working too hard to take any notice. I hold my hands up for that mistake," and he smiled with sadness at the thought.

"Anyway Doreen, Mrs. Stevens, congratulations. Tell me what about your sister. Are you going to tell her?" asked Tommy.

"Oh," cried Doreen, "We have already done so; this morning. She is extremely happy for us, and is going to move into a small bungalow on the estate so she can be near me; near us," and again she turned to smile warmly at her husband.

"Well, that's good news. Once again, my congratulations. I will let the police know that you are safe," he said, rising from his chair ready to show them the door.

As they both rose, Tommy asked, "What about your son, Mr. Stevens. To be honest he doesn't strike me as the sort of person who is going to take to you having a young wife."

Ronald looked at his wife before laughing and replying, "No, Mr. Doyle, you are right he isn't. But at the end of the day, he gets on with his life, and I get on with mine. Besides, he knows better than to cross me. You see, I still hold the purse strings, and very tightly I can assure you. The question is, how long his wife will put up with his behaviour. If she kicks him out, where do you think he's going to want to live," and he smiled warmly holding out his hand to shake Doyle's.

"By the way, Mr. Doyle, I understand payment is due for the time you've spent searching for Doreen. Please accept this," and Mr. Stevens passed him an envelope.

Quickly opening the envelope Tommy was surprised at how generous the amount was, saying, "This is too much, Mr. Stevens. My terms are $50 a day plus expenses."

"No worries," replied Stevens. "The extra is for putting the fear of God in my son. You got him worried when you mentioned Doreen might have been murdered; you really did frighten him. He doesn't like you, Mr. Doyle," and he laughed warmly at the thought.

After they had left Tommy put a quick call into Mac, explaining about Doreen and Stevens Senior. Mac laughed, thanking Tommy for closing the case.

Then he rang Mrs. Dobson, who sounded excited and pleased with the happy news. When Doyle got a word in, he asked, "Do you know what happened to the letter, Mrs. Dobson?"

There was an intake of breath before Marcia timidly admitted, "Oh yes, Mr. Doyle. I am so sorry. It was my fault entirely. I picked the letter up one morning, just as I was leaving for work, and slipped it into my coat pocket. Somewhere along the journey, it must have dropped out, and I forgot all about it. I feel so stupid."

Doyle laughed, before apologising for doing so. Marcia laughed too. "Not worry, Mr. Doyle. Oh, by the way, what about your bill? Will you send it to me please?"

Tommy coughed. "Err… it's all been taken care of, Mrs. Dobson. Mr. Stevens has settled the account. He feels he is more to blame than Doreen. Anyway, the case is now closed; both with me and the police. Have a happy life. Goodbye, Mrs. Dobson."

Reluctantly, Marcia responded, "I will. Now I have another family member. I know Doreen will be looked after, and I don't have to worry about her anymore. Good-bye, Mr. Doyle. It was a pleasure to meet you."

'I bet it was,' thought Tommy, as he placed the phone back on the receiver.

Taking up the Doreen Smith file, he wrote across it Case Closed.

'At least that was a happy ending!' thought Tommy as he filed the folder away.

THE COLUMBO EFFECT

The blazing sirens and flashing lights Dragged Tommy from a deep sleep. It took him a few moments to realise what it was that had woken him.

By the time he had fully surfaced the vehicles had passed by and peace reigned once more outside the brownstone building of his home. Sitting up, he flicked the switch on the light sitting on his nightstand. The clock said five-forty.

Sighing he threw back the covers and climbed out of bed. He was wide awake now and knew he wouldn't get back to sleep. Grabbing a sweater, he ambled towards the kitchen switching on the coffee pot. In the distance, he could hear more sirens.

'Must be a big 'un,' he thought, going to the lounge window to look outside - but he saw nothing. Shrugging his shoulders, he returned to the kitchen to pour himself a cup of coffee. The smell of the dark black brew assailed his nostrils. Taking a sip, it was hot. Then he took another sip, quickly feeling its reviving effect.

Heading back into the lounge Tommy flopped down onto the settee. Picking up the remote he turned on the TV and started clicking through the channels; stopping when he came across a re-run of an old Colombo episode.

Funnily, the character was one of his favourites. Tommy sometimes felt a little akin to the TV detective, admiring how he worked; always questioning, making sure he never forgot the smallest point. The detective always managed to get his man; or in this case woman. The last Tommy remembered was Columbo arresting the culprit; another job well done.

Sometime later, resurfacing from his dozing, Tommy stood up. He stretched, feeling the aches and pains of his years. Not that he was old but still, sleeping on the settee was not the most comfortable of places.

Once dressed, he went downstairs to his office to check the answerphone; there were no messages. 'Good,' he thought, 'it's gonna be a quiet day.'

Suddenly the ring of the doorbell echoed around the quiet office. Checking his security screen Tommy saw the postman standing on the doorstep. Pressing the button to open the front door, he allowed the man to slip inside. Going to the top of the stairs he watched as the inner door closed and the postman mounted the stairs.

"Morning, Mr. Doyle," announced Steve. "Got a package for you."

"Do you want a drink, Steve?" asked Tommy. "I've just made some coffee."

Placing the package on the desk the postman thanked him; accepting a cup of black coffee, he sat down on a chair by the desk. "Did you hear about the fire last night?" he asked. "It was bad."

"Yea; the sirens woke me, sometime before six. Where was it?" responded Tommy.

"Two blocks down," replied Steve, feeling pleased that he was the first to give the investigator the news. "Very bad it is. Nearly took a whole block out; practically destroyed the mini market."

Tommy looked up in surprise. "The Italian one?"

"That's the one. Poor Marco was seriously injured and is in hospital," responded the man. Rising he made for the door, before continuing, "It's a shame really; I feel sorry for Carlotta, Marco's wife, she has nowhere to stay at the moment."

"Was she hurt in the fire?" asked Tommy.

"No. She had gone down the street to O'Malley's to help Molly in the kitchen; they have a big wedding tomorrow so they were getting everything ready. It seems both Carlotta and Marco offered to help but he went back to the shop early," Steve continued as he headed for the stairs. "Fortunately, the kids stayed overnight at a friend's house; lucky, weren't they?"

"Sure were. Where's Carlotta and the kids at the moment," questioned Tommy.

The postman stopped halfway down the staircase, and turning to look up at Tommy, he replied, "I'm not sure. Perhaps they're with the O' Malley's. See you later Mr. Doyle; thanks for the coffee." Opening the inner door, he let himself out of the brownstone, waving as he went.

Tommy returned to his office and picking up the phone he rang his pal at the precinct.

"Hey, Tommy, and what can I do for you?" asked Mac in his broad Scottish brogue.

"Morning, Mac. You hear about the fire at Marco's Mini Market?"

There was a short pause while Mac checked the records. "Yea, a bad one that; practically destroyed the place. Err, why the interest Tommy?"

"Just heard about it. I was woken up by the sirens but didn't realise it was to do with them. Anyway, I was wondering what had happened to Carlotta and the kids and how Marco is doing?" Tommy asked.

Mac sighed, "Sorry Tommy, but Marco's in a bad way. The doctors are not sure if he will make it or not. As for Carlotta, the last I heard the O' Malley's were looking after her and the kids. At the moment, it's arson but, if Marco doesn't make it, then it gets shot up to murder. Are you thinking of looking into the matter, Tommy?"

Doyle thought for a moment, then he said, "I thought I might check around and see what I can find out. Any problem with me doing that, Mac?"

Mac laughed down the receiver, saying, "Since when have I had a problem with you, Tommy lad. Keep me posted if you come up with anything, okay."

"Yea; sure will. Talk to you later," and Tommy hung up the receiver.

Half an hour later, Tommy strolled into O'Malley's Bar & Diner to speak to Molly O' Malley. After spending some time with her he discovered that Carlotta and her kids had gone to the hospital to see Marco. Molly explained that at the moment they were staying with her and Pat as their boys were away. However, the lads were due back in a couple of days so she wasn't sure where Carlotta would go after that. Tommy told her not to worry about it, that he would sort something out.

Leaving the bar, Tommy drove to the hospital wondering what had been the reason for the fire. Why had they targeted Marco; he wouldn't harm a fly. He was an up-front type of guy, often giving people a few days' credit when things got tough.

The fact it might be arson surprised Tommy. He hoped this was a one-off incident, and not the start of something more serious. The district had been peaceful and law-abiding for well over three years, so he was concerned that it might be the start of a crime spree. The thought would disturb his nights.

Arriving at the hospital, Tommy quickly found the burns unit where the injured man was being kept. Walking into the room he was shocked to see Marco bandaged from head to foot and on a life support machine. Carlotta was sitting by the bedside. She looked up as Tommy walked in, relief crossing her face.

"Mr. Doyle!" Carlotta announced. "Thank you for coming."

Tommy bent down to peck her cheek before asking, "How is he, Lottie?" That was Tommy's pet name for the lovely Italian woman.

She smiled weakly, trying to show some strength but obviously stunned by what had happened. Eventually, she spoke. "He's holding his own at the moment. The Doctors are trying to be positive but I can see they are worried about him. Oh, Mr. Doyle, I am so afraid. I don't know what we are going to do."

Sitting down in a chair next to her he took hold of her hand, saying soothingly, "Now, now, Lottie, I don't want you to worry. I'll take care of everything. You just concentrate on Marco. By the way where are the kids?"

Carlotta smiled at him before saying, "Mr. Doyle, you are so kind. The kids are at school. It's better for them; this way they are amongst their friends and it'll keep their minds occupied."

Tommy and Carlotta sat quietly for a while, listening to the noise of the breathing machine keeping poor Marco alive. Finally, he said, "Molly tells me you're staying at their place for the moment but that the boys will be home soon; do you have any plans for when they get back?"

She looked up at him, shaking her head no, as he continued speaking, "Well, what do you say about coming to stay in my top floor apartment until we can sort something permanent out for you. Would you like to do that, Lottie?"

Carlotta turned her head to look at Doyle, relief spreading across her face as she responded, "Oh, Mr. Doyle, do you mean it. Could we stay in the apartment? Are you sure we won't be a nuisance," and she smiled?

Smiling back, Tommy took her hand again, "Now, Lottie, when have you ever been a nuisance. Of course, it's no problem. The apartment is ready to move in too, it has everything you need and there's enough room for you and the kids. And I'm sure Marco would approve. Okay."

Tears sprang into Carlotta's eyes which she quickly dashed away, knowing Tommy was uncomfortable with teary women. Once she had calmed herself, she smiled warmly at him, saying, "You are so kind, Mr. Doyle. Thank you so very much. That will make it a lot easier for us. And I am sure Marco will be happy knowing we are somewhere safe."

Rising, he announced, "Listen, Lottie, I have to go and sort a few things out. Here's my mobile number." And Tommy handed her one of his business cards. "When you're ready to leave give me a ring and I'll be back to pick you up."

As he started to leave the room he stopped, and turning back, asked her, "Do you have any money? You might need to do some shopping; you know for clothes and things?"

Carlotta smiled at Doyle, replying that she was okay. She had been in touch with the bank and they had been very helpful but thanked him warmly for his consideration. Waving, Tommy left. His first stop was the mini market, then he was off to see Mac.

As Doyle entered the police precinct, he found himself being acknowledged by a number of the ex-colleagues he had worked with for many years. He always felt at home whenever he came to the precinct. Mounting the stairs to the detective's office, Doyle looked for Mac; Inspector Pete Mackintosh, his former partner of over fifteen years.

"Whoa there, Tommy, how are Marco and Carlotta doing?" asked Mac.

Tommy sat down on the spare chair near Mac's desk, before answering, "He's still poorly, but Lottie's trying to keep her spirits up. I've offered her and the kids the upstairs apartment at my place until things get sorted. Any update on the fire?"

Mac smiled. He knew how fond Tommy was of the Italian couple, as they had been the first people to welcome Doyle when he moved into the district. The mini-market was also Doyle's closest food store.

Eventually, Mac said, "Not much more than I told you earlier. It was definitely arson. Looks like

63

someone poured a very powerful accelerant through a back window. The window was barred but whoever did it, broke the glass first to pour the liquid in. There must have been a hell of a lot of it because it caught fire pretty quickly."

"Hell," said Tommy, before allowing Mac to continue.

"From what we can gather, Marco got up early with Carlotta," Mac read from his report. "The kids had stayed overnight at their friends as they were supposed to be going straight to school from there. Marco went with Carlotta to O' Malley's for a bite to eat, then he decided to return to the store to catch up on some paperwork. The fire officer says there was quite a bit of flammable stuff in the basement and that the fire must have been burning for some time. Whatever was stored beneath the old gas pipe must have burned slowly and strongly; the heat from it caused the pipe to fracture. It went up just as Marco returned to the store. He didn't stand a chance; he got caught in the blast. After that, the whole lot went up. Unfortunately, the Sixth Street Bridge was closed so it took longer for the emergency services to arrive."

"Ah, that's why I heard them come past my place. Poor Marco; wrong place, wrong time," announced Tommy. "Presumably there were no witnesses."

Mac shook his head, saying, "No. The arsonist chose the most opportunistic time to hit. If they hadn't got up early, then both of them could have ended up hurt; maybe killed. I'm not sure they would have stood a chance of getting out."

Tommy shook his head in agreement.

Rising, he thanked Mac, telling him he would keep in touch, and with that, he quickly left the precinct. Perhaps when he spoke to Carlotta later, she might be able to give him some idea as to why they had been targeted, although he doubted it.

Arriving back at the hospital Tommy found Carlotta ready and waiting for him. Their first point of call was to a few local shops so she could buy some new clothing, and some food for her and the kids. The next stop was to collect the kids from school before driving back to Tommy's brownstone building.

Once inside he showed his visitors around the upstairs apartment and left them to settle in. An hour later a timid knock at his office door made Tommy look up from what he was doing. Calling out 'enter' the door opened and he saw Carlotta standing in the doorway, hesitating to enter.

"Sorry to disturb you, Mr. Doyle but I wondered if you would care to join us for a meal," she tentatively asked.

Tommy was surprised by the invitation, "You don't have to feed me, Lottie, you know, and you should call me Tommy, you've known me long enough now," and he smiled to show he was teasing her.

"I know, Mr. Doyle, Tommy I mean, but I have made a meal so you are welcome to join us. There is plenty," responded Carlotta.

Tommy smiled warmly at her, responding, "Thank you, I would be delighted to join you for a meal. What time do you want me upstairs?"

Carlotta breathed a sigh of relief. Unbeknown to Tommy she felt very obligated to him for his kindness. And, she didn't want to be seen to be taking advantage of his generosity. She hesitated as if reluctant to leave, so he asked, "Is there a problem, Lottie? Do you want something else?"

"I wondered, err I wondered if I could use the phone to ring the hospital," she asked.

Tommy quickly stood up, "Of course. I forgot the phone upstairs isn't connected. I'll get that sorted out for you tomorrow. Here use this one. Give this number to the hospital. If they ring before the other phone is connected, I'll let you know," and he moved away from the desk to allow her access to the phone.

Later that evening, after a delightful meal, Tommy left Carlotta and the family to get a peaceful night. Tomorrow was another day; hopefully, there would be some good news from the hospital.

* * * *

The next morning, Tommy was up and about earlier than normal, probably due to having people in the upstairs flat. Or, more likely, because he had slept on the pull-out bed in his office. He had been working for half an hour when he heard the two youngsters leave for school.

Ten minutes later a knock at his door heralded the arrival of Carlotta. He called enter and waited. Opening the door Carlotta, seeing him watching her, smiled, "I'm off to the hospital to see how Marco is doing okay."

Tommy smiled back and standing, announced, "Let me run you over there. We can talk on the way. I have a couple of questions I need to ask you if that's okay?"

Nodding her head, she agreed to his suggestion, as long as it wasn't putting him out. He told her not to worry. Ten minutes later they were on their way.

After a short silence, he asked her, "Have you any idea who might have done this?"

She looked at him, thinking about it before responding, "No. I can't believe it's happened and I have no clue as to why someone would do this to us. We get on with everybody in the neighbourhood."

Tommy asked, "There's hasn't been anyone who Marco might have refused to serve, or who hasn't paid what they owe? No cross words; no one threatening Marco or you in any way?"

Carlotta was silent for a moment, obviously trying to remember if there had been someone. Finally, she replied, "Honestly Mr. Doyle, Tommy, I cannot think of anyone who would want to harm my poor Marco," and she started to weep as she remembered the sight of her husband lying in the hospital bed.

Tommy felt a little uncomfortable. 'Damn," he thought. He hadn't meant to upset her.

By the time he pulled the car into the hospital car park, Carlotta had gained control of her emotions. He was relieved. Entering the burns unit, they were met by the Doctor. For a moment both Tommy and

Carlotta panicked; afraid that they were about to hear the worst news.

The Doctor suddenly smiled, reassuringly announcing that Marco was awake. This was the last thing they had expected. He was still very poorly but it was a good sign. With constant care and time, Marco would recover from the fire although he would carry the scars forever.

Entering the hospital room, Carlotta and Doyle saw a very different scene than the one they had left the previous day. Marco's eyes were open and as they approached the bed, he very slowly moved his hand in recognition. The look of love that passed between the couple was something Doyle was envious of.

Sitting down by the side of the bed, Tommy watched as Marco turned to look at him trying to speak.

Holding up his hand, Tommy said, "It's alright, Marco, don't try and talk; at least not yet. Carlotta and the kids are staying at my place. I'm keeping an eye on them, so they are safe. Don't you worry about them, okay?"

Marco blinked his eyes in acknowledgment. If he hadn't been bandaged Tommy would have seen a smile and the look of relief etched across the man's face.

Leaning towards her husband, Carlotta gently said, "Mr. Doyle, Tommy, has been very kind by offering us his upstairs apartment."

"And they can stay as long as necessary," interrupted Doyle. "So, no worries there either." Marco blinked his eyes, nodding his head ever so slightly to show he understood and agreed.

Tommy decided it would be better to leave the couple alone for a short while, saying he was going to ring Mac and tell him the good news about Marco being awake. Quickly, he left the room.

Fifteen minutes later, Tommy returned, arranging a time to collect Carlotta as he was off to meet Mac at the mini-market, so would call back for her later. At his comment, Marco turned his head to look at him. There was a questioning look in his eyes.

Tommy understood what it was he was trying to ask. Slowly Tommy moved his head from side to side. Marco understood. His business had gone up in flames which saddened him.

Arriving at the mini-market Tommy was not surprised to see it was black and wet. The fire brigade had poured a lot of water into the building in order to control the blaze. What the fire hadn't destroyed, the water had ruined.

"What a mess," announced Mac as Tommy joined him inside the building.

Tommy looked around before responding, "No clues I suppose."

"As it happens, Tommy, there is. We've discovered a can in a dumpster three blocks down the street. Forensics thinks it might have contained the stuff used to light the fire," declared Mac.

"Any fingerprints?" Doyle was pleased that at least the investigation was picking up some clues.

"Not yet, but it's gone to be tested. Sorry, we'll just have to wait. Any news on Marco" asked Mac.

Tommy smiled. "Yea, he's conscious. But in pain of course, but at least the Doctor thinks he's passed the first milestone. Gonna be a long recovery process though."

Mac smiled. He was pleased by the news. "Have you found anything out yet, Tommy?"

Tommy shook his head. "No. I asked Carlotta but she couldn't think of one person who would want to harm them. She's as flummoxed by the whole thing as we are."

Mac sighed. He hated jobs like this; no clues, no witnesses, and therefore, no suspects; what the hell was going on. This was a quiet, trouble-free neighbourhood so what was happening. The two guys decided to leave the damaged market and stroll down the street to O' Malley's Bar & Diner to have a bite to eat. As they left the damaged building a voice called out, "Tommy, Mr. Doyle, have you got a minute please?"

Turning towards the sound, they discovered Janice Bartholomew coming towards them. Tommy stopped and waited for her to catch up with him.

Janice owned the office next door to the mini-market. She was an accountant and looked after a lot of the local businesses which had sprung up over the last couple of years.

Catching up with him she breathlessly asked, "Tommy, I wanted to ask a big favour, please. I was out of town when this happened, "and she spread her arm around to indicate the fire-damaged building, before continuing speaking, "I only got back this morning but I find that there is a lot of smoke damage in my part of the building."

"Sorry to hear that, Janice," responded Tommy. "Is it very bad?"

Janice smiled warmly, "Actually the place stinks something awful, and there's been some water damage, so unfortunately I'm not going to be able to work in there. Also, the fire chief tells me he thinks the wall between the market and my office may not be very safe. I need to get out what I can and move. I wondered if your apartment was free to rent."

Doyle shook his head. "Sorry Janice, but Carlotta and the kids are staying in it."

Janice looked disappointed. "Oh, well of course I understand. That's okay, I suppose I will have to try and find somewhere else," and she started to walk away.

Doyle thought for a moment, then suddenly announced, "Hang on, Janice. The two offices downstairs are empty. If you can get some temporary furniture, you could use one as an office and the other as an apartment. There are kitchen and bathroom facilities in both."

Janice smiled, delighted by the suggestion, and quickly leaning forward she pecked Tommy on the cheek, declaring, "You're a life saver, Tommy Doyle. I'm sure I can sort some things out."

Doyle blushed ever so slightly, much to the amusement of Mac, who wondered if his pal had a thing for the lady. Fortunately, Doyle didn't see the glint in Mac's eyes or he might have changed his mind about letting Janice use the offices. As it was, he was busy fiddling with his key chain, removing the spare key to give it to Janice so she could gain access to the building while he was running Carlotta about. Having given her the key and code for the alarm system he waved aside Janice's exuberant thanks, saying, "I'll catch up with you later," and turning back towards Mac, they continued walking down the street.

Mac couldn't resist commenting. "Very nice lady that Janice, ain't she, Tommy?"

Doyle cast a quick sideways glance at Mac, before agreeing she was a nice lady. Nothing more was said as they made their way down the street to O' Malley's bar.

Molly and Pat O' Malley were delighted with the news of Marco being awake. Molly declared she would go and visit him as soon as she could. Tommy suggested she call round to the apartment later on and speak to Carlotta first, which she readily agreed to do.

The pair sat down to enjoy a light lunch and a general chat with the O' Malley's. With lunch over Tommy said goodbye to Mac and returned to the hospital to collect Carlotta. The kids were delighted when their Mother told them about their Father being awake. It was agreed they could 'bunk off' school the following day to spend time with him.

That evening when they returned to the brownstone building Tommy noted Janice had moved in. Knocking on her door he checked she had everything she needed. As he retired for the evening, he thought what a full house it was, something he had not had for quite a while.

* * * *

Over the next few days, Marco slowly improved until finally the bandage around his face was removed and he was free to speak, albeit in a whisper.

Tuesday morning it was raining quite heavily so Tommy Dropped Carlotta outside the hospital before parking the car and then following her inside. As he passed the reception desk, he overheard someone having a conversation with the receptionist. Normally he would have ignored such things, except hearing Marco's name being mentioned, caused his senses to liven. By the time it registered with him and he had turned around, whoever had enquired about Marco had quickly disappeared.

Approaching the receptionist, he questioned her, "Hi, I'm Tommy Doyle," and he flashed his PI card. "Did I just overhear someone asking about Marco?"

The receptionist looked up and seeing a good-looking man staring at her, she smiled warmly. "Yes. A young person was asking for information on the state of Mr. Beneto. I said I couldn't give out such information, only to immediate family."

"What did he say to that," asked Tommy.

"Not much," replied the receptionist. "He just wanted to know if he was going to die."

Tommy was surprised. Thinking about it he then asked the receptionist, "Was the person male or female, and do you think you would recognise him again?"

The receptionist wondered about the questioning, so leaning forward, she looked Tommy in the eyes, replying, "Male. A young man; probably about 17 or 18 years old. And yes, I think I would recognise him again. Why?"

Tommy pondered for a moment before replying, "Because, we need to tell the police. That may be the person who caused the fire which nearly killed Mr. Beneto. I'll give them a ring and they'll send a sketch artist down to speak to you," and with that, he turned away to call Mac to explain what had just happened.

Two hours later Mac and Tommy were stood in the hospital corridor chatting about nothing much. They were waiting for the police sketch artist to finish creating a composite of the young man who had made inquiries regarding Marco earlier in the day. Both of them were impatient for the job to be done. This could be the first major lead into who had carried out the arson attack.

Finally, the sketch was finished. As they looked at the picture Mac and Tommy saw the face of a youngster staring back at them. He was aged about eighteen years old. Neither recognised him. Taking the ID picture through into Marco's room they showed it to the couple hoping they would recognise the person. They drew a blank; neither knew the young man. They were deflated but at least they had more than before; not much maybe, but still it was a lead.

"Hey Mac, do you think I could have a copy of that. I could show it to some of the local kids; they might recognise the face," asked Tommy.

"Sure, no problem," said Mac and he disappeared into the hospital's office, returning five minutes later with a copy of the picture he had photocopied.

"Thanks," said Tommy pocketing the picture. He had an idea who he was going to talk to about the image. Mac was happy to let him do so, as he knew Tommy would probably get more answers than the beat cops would. Kids were sometimes very suspicious of the police.

Over the next few days, life in the brownstone settled into a comfortable routine. Janice and Carlotta took turns in offering Doyle dinner each evening. Sometimes, he would accept their kind invitations, other times he would make his excuses and leave the building.

Janice had soon got the two offices ship-shape. She had rented some furniture and quickly got herself into a routine. There were few visitors to the building, as she tended to visit her clients' premises when working. Luckily, she had managed to salvage her computer, client records, and some of her stuff. A lot would have to be thrown away as the smoke damage was too great. But at least the wall between her office and the mini-market had remained standing, having eventually being given the all-clear.

Marco slowly improved and began to talk normally. Carlotta went to see him every day, as did other people from the community.

Doyle in the meantime spent his spare time strolling around the neighbourhood trying to discover who the mysterious young man was. So far, he had had no luck. Which could mean he wasn't local but more likely someone from out of the area. This concerned Doyle.

To cover as many people as he could Doyle had taken extra copies of the image, creating a 'wanted' style poster. He had approached all the businesses in the area asking them to place the poster somewhere obvious, in the hope that someone would recognise the face. But, so far with no luck.

By the time Sunday morning came around again, Marco had been in hospital for four weeks. Carlotta had left early that morning to go to church before continuing on to the hospital to see her husband. He could talk much more now, and he had also started eating again. She had taken him some soup, believing a bit of home cooking would do him the world of good. Doyle thought she was right, as her cooking had certainly done him good. She had continued cooking for him, mainly because each time she offered to pay rent for the apartment he had told her no. The relief she felt was immense. Both her and Marco would be eternally grateful to Doyle for all his assistance.

Sitting in his office, Doyle was mulling over what his next move should be in trying to find the young man. It had been nearly two weeks now and there had been no response to the posters. Suddenly, there was a soft knocking at his door. Doyle's head shot up at the sound. It had to be one of Carlotta's kids, as both their Mother and Janice were out, so he called, "Come in."

The door slowly opened and Angelo poked his head around the door. "Can I come in, Mr. Doyle?"

Tommy waved him in. Pointing at the chair, he indicated he should sit down, "Good morning, Angelo, and what can I do for you?"

The young man chose to walk around the office rather than sit. He didn't answer immediately so Tommy waited. He felt the young man had something to say but perhaps he wasn't sure how to start. Stopping in front of the poster Angelo stared at the image of the young man. Tommy stood up, slowly going to stand alongside him.

"Do you recognise him, Angelo?" Tommy asked quietly.

The young man didn't answer. Tommy remained silent, waiting until Angelo made up his mind to speak.

Finally, the boy asked, "Do you think the police will catch him?"

Tommy didn't answer immediately, eventually, saying, "I'm not sure; maybe. At the moment, they have no clue as to who he is. I think they're hoping that someone will come forward with a name. What I do know is, that he needs to be caught. Having committed arson once means he could do it again, and next time someone could die. Your father was extremely lucky."

Returning to his seat, he asked, "Have you had breakfast yet, Angelo."

The young man looked up in surprise. "No."

"How do you fancy going with me to the cafe for some bacon and eggs? Perhaps we can chat a bit more; you can tell me how school is doing?"

Angelo looked at Tommy. Finally, he agreed, and the pair of them left the brownstone heading down the street to Jacko's Cafe.

Once they had ordered breakfast, Tommy began asking Angelo about his school, making general conversation, allowing the young man to relax. It proved to work. Angelo responded by telling Tommy about a funny incident that had occurred a couple of weeks previous.

After breakfast, the pair strolled back towards the brownstone chatting. "Mr. Doyle, what's going to happen to the mini market," Angelo asked.

Tommy looked at him. "What do you mean happen?"

Angelo explained that if the mini market was ruined and his father wasn't going to be able to work then he wondered what would happen to the family.

Tommy explained that he was sure his mother and father would work something out so he wasn't to worry; just concentrate on doing well at school and making his parents proud of him.

Angelo didn't respond.

Arriving back at the brownstone the young man thanked Tommy for breakfast, quickly returning to the top floor apartment without saying another word. Tommy returned to his office deep in thought, 'There is one troubled young man.'

That evening, Tommy was out with the guys playing cards at Mac's place. As the evening progressed, they ended up discussing the missing young man in the poster.

"Someone should know him," announced Curly (Charles Denver, Desk Sergeant).

Mac played his cards before answering, "The problem is he's not local. It may be that we have to widen the search. What about the mini market, Tommy; do you know what Marco is going to do with it?"

Doyle shook his head, before answering, "He hasn't got a clue. Besides he needs to concentrate on getting better before he decides on the future."

The evening ended about eleven-thirty and it was just past midnight when Tommy finally got back to his apartment. Mounting the stairs to the second floor he suddenly came across Angelo asleep on the landing. Quietly and gently, Tommy touched him to wake him up, thinking, 'Now what the hell is he doing there.'

Angelo opened his eyes.

"Are you waiting for me, Angelo?"

The young man nodded his head.

"Come into my office so we can talk," said Tommy unlocking the door and leading the way inside. "You should be in bed fast asleep, not sitting in a cold stairway. Does your Mother know where you are?"

The young man shook his head, indicating she didn't, so Tommy asked, "Do you want a warm drink?"

Angelo nodded his head. "Please," before sitting down on the settee while Tommy went into the kitchen to put the kettle on. A few moments later he returned to the lounge with two steaming mugs; one of coffee and one of cocoa. The latter he passed to Angelo before sitting down in an easy chair. "So, what would you like to talk to me about?" he asked.

Angelo said nothing, his head was bent as he was not sure where to start. Finally, he blurted out, "I know who that boy is. He did it because of me. I caused my dad to be burnt," and he burst into tears.

Tommy looked up surprised. "Now, what do you mean you caused your dad to be burnt?"

Eventually, Angelo stopped crying; sniffing he wiped his face on his sleeve. He took a couple of hesitant breaths before letting the whole sorry tale pour out.

And pour out it did. Ten minutes later he went quiet, looking at the floor, ashamed at what he felt he had done wrong. He sat waiting for Tommy to tear him to pieces.

After a moment or two Tommy said, "Firstly, it isn't your fault what happened to your father and the mini market."

Angelo's head shot up as he cried out, "But if I'd done what Liam Murphy asked me to do then he wouldn't have burnt the market down, would he?"

"You don't know that. Besides, what he wanted you to do was wrong. Do you think your father would have been happy if you had got caught and been arrested?"

Angelo shook his head. He knew Doyle was right. His father would never have forgiven him if he had gotten arrested but would he forgive him for what had happened now?

Tommy could see the fight Angelo was having with himself over the whole affair. He realised the young man felt guilty that his father had got hurt. But what Tommy wanted him to realise was that he wasn't to blame for the actions of this Murphy person. The other boy was the one who had done wrong. He would speak to Mac first thing in the morning and see if they could get the mess sorted. In the meantime, he should get Angelo upstairs and off to bed.

"Okay, Angelo, you did the right thing by not doing what this Murphy guy wanted you to do. You've also done right by telling me everything. What I want you to do now is go to bed and leave everything to me. I'll speak to the police tomorrow, and then I'll talk to your parents. It's going to be alright. So, off you go and get a good night's sleep. We'll talk again tomorrow, okay."

Angelo stood up; relief flowing over him that he had finally got the whole sorry story of his chest. "Thank you, Mr. Doyle, for letting me talk to you," he said holding out his hand to shake Doyle's.

Taking hold of the young man's hand, Tommy shook it. "Thank you, for trusting me. You know you can come and talk to me anytime, and if I can help you, I will. Now off to bed and no worrying about it, okay." Angelo nodded and running up the stairs he quietly let himself into the top floor apartment.

Tommy closed his door and turning out the light he retired for the night.

* * * *

The following morning, Tommy was up and working in his office by seven o'clock. He had rung Mac at six-thirty and told him who the young man in the composite picture was. He was now waiting for Mac to ring him back to let him know they had arrested Murphy.

The phone rang at eight-thirty. It was Mac, "Just to let you know, we have him in custody. At the moment, we are waiting for the young man's lawyer. We will need Angelo to come down to the station to make a statement. Can you bring him in, Tommy?"

Tommy replied he would, and after putting the phone receiver down he went upstairs to collect Angelo.

Half an hour later they arrived at the precinct. Sitting with Mac, Angelo explained what had happened with Liam Murphy. Mac took a statement from him, after which he was allowed to leave.

Dropping him off at school, Tommy told Angelo not to worry; he would see him later in the afternoon. He then returned to the precinct to listen in on the interview with Murphy.

As was to be expected the young man denied having anything to do with Angelo or the fire at the mini-market. When questioned as to why he was enquiring about Marco if he didn't know the family, the young man denied being at the hospital.

Mac had eventually put him in a line-up and the hospital receptionist had identified him. Despite this, he continued to deny ever being at the hospital until Mac sprung on him two photographs; one of him entering, and one of him leaving the hospital. He finally capitulated, confessing that he had been there, but only out of curiosity.

It took another two hours of questioning before he finally confessed to setting the fire at the mini-market. He declared it was his way of getting back at Angelo because he wouldn't agree to do what he had asked him to do. The case was closed with Liam Murphy being charged with arson, causing grievous bodily harm, and attempted murder. Both Mac and Tommy were highly satisfied with the outcome.

Happy with the results Tommy knew he had to put Angelo out of his misery, and smooth things over with his family, so he headed straight for the hospital. When he arrived, he was pleasantly surprised to discover Marco sitting up in bed. Carlotta and he were laughing at some private joke, leaving him feeling a little uncomfortable at disturbing them.

"Mr. Doyle, Tommy, what a pleasure to see you, please come in," requested Marco.

Tommy smiled before sitting down. "How you doing, Marco. You look a lot better today."

Marco nodded his head, "I feel a lot better."

Carlotta looked at Tommy. "Do you have some news, Tommy?"

'She's very perceptive,' thought Tommy before answering her. "As it happens, I do. They've caught the arsonist, and he's confessed all."

Carlotta blurted out, "Really. You know this for sure?"

Tommy looked at her smiling, replying, "I do. I've just come from the precinct. He's been charged with three offenses."

Both Carlotta and Marco were delighted with the news, wanting to know everything that Tommy could tell them, which he did.

"What I don't understand," stated Marco "Is why he did it. We don't know him so why us?"

Doyle wondered how much to tell them. The whole story would have to come out eventually. Would it be better to tell it now, or later?

He decided now, and so began explaining why Murphy had done what he had. "Murphy is not a nice young man, and unfortunately he decided to try to get Angelo into trouble."

"Angelo," Carlotta almost yelled. "What has he got to do with Angelo?"

"Shush, Carlotta, let Mr. Doyle continue" responded Marco. "Go on, Tommy, please tell us everything."

Doyle nodded his head and continued speaking, "This Murphy character wanted Angelo to steal some cigarettes and booze from the mini-market. When Angelo refused, he got a bit pushy and they ended up fighting."

"I remember that," stated Carlotta. "He came home one day, dirty and bruised. He told me they had been playing football or something in the park, and when I pushed him about it, he said the other team had got a bit rough. I believed him."

"But he didn't steal did he, Mr. Doyle?" asked Marco.

Tommy shook his head. "No, Marco, he didn't. You have a very good son there. He refused point-blank, and when Murphy threatened to burn the place down, he didn't believe him. Now he regrets not telling you. He blames himself for you being caught in the fire, and for being injured. I think he has had quite a few sleepless nights ever since."

Marco sighed, "Poor Angelo. It wasn't his fault. I don't blame him for the fire. I'm so proud that he didn't do wrong. Will you tell him, Tommy, that I am not cross with him? I'm only sorry that he didn't feel able to come and tell me about the problem."

"He'll probably be calling in on his way home from school, why don't you tell him then, yourself," suggested Tommy. "Shall I call back for you Lottie?"

Carlotta smiled. "No, that's okay, Tommy. I'll wait for Angelo and we'll get a cab back. Thank you."

Tommy nodded, and waving goodbye he left the couple to discuss their son.

On his way back home, Doyle called in at O' Malley's for a bite to eat.

"Hello, Tommy," Pat called out as he entered the bar. "Want something to eat? Oh, by the way, Molly wants a word with you before you go; something to do with Carlotta and Marco."

Doyle acknowledged the request before going to sit at a table in the corner. Looking at the menu he decided to order his usual; Molly's famous Stew and Dumplings. He was looking forward to the meal.

Later, once he had eaten, and Molly had finished cooking, she came to join him at the table. As she sat down, he asked, "And how are you, Molly dear?"

She smiled at him. "I'm okay, Tommy. And how is Marco doing?"

"He's doing fine. Sitting up and talking okay now."

Molly smiled again, pleased. "That's good news. Now, Tommy, I want to talk to you about the mini-market. I've been talking to some of the neighbours, and we think it needs sorting. So, we were wondering what we could do to help?"

"Such as?" enquired Tommy interested in what she was saying.

"Well," began Molly. "What we thought of doing was to clean the place up, repair it, and to get it ship-shape for when Marco comes out of the hospital. What do you think, Tommy?"

Doyle smiled in response. "I think that sounds brilliant. What do you want from me?"

Molly clapped her hands with joy, declaring, "We need you to keep Carlotta away from the market until it's done. If she wants to go there, can you try and make sure she doesn't?"

"I will do all I can to assist. Mind you at the moment she spends most of her days at the hospital. If you need anything else you let me know. Have you started a fund towards the cost of it all?"

Molly nodded her head. "Yes, we have. It's amazing how many people have contributed cash, as well as committing their time to the project. Aren't people wonderful?" and she quickly wiped the tears that had sprung in her eyes at the thought of it all.

Tommy leant over to give her a comforting hug. "You're a big softy, Molly O' Malley but you're also a little gem. Call around later and I'll give you some money for the fund. Sorry, but I've got to go. Remember, let me know if you need anything else? Okay?" And standing he gave Molly a peck on the cheek, saluted Pat, and quickly left the diner to return home.

* * * *

Five weeks later Tommy and Carlotta arrived at the hospital ready to collect Marco. He was being allowed home on strict instructions that he was to take it steady for another few weeks. His burns had proven not to be as bad as the doctors had at first thought, so his recovery had been much quicker than expected. Carlotta had been shown how to change his dressings until he returned to the hospital at the end of the month.

Doyle's main concern with Marco coming home had been him having to go up the stairs to the apartment. Carlotta had also been worried about this so she had arranged for the whole family to go and stay with her cousin on the other side of the city. They lived in a very large dormer-style bungalow so there was enough space for one of the downstairs rooms to be converted into a bedroom for them, with the kids sleeping upstairs.

The hospital arranged for an ambulance to take Marco to the bungalow, whilst Doyle drove the rest of the family and their belongings. Once he had seen them safely settled in, he made his goodbyes and returned home.

Turning the corner of the block he came upon the mini-market. Seeing several vehicles parked in the car park he parked his car. Entering the market, he looked around for Molly. She was up a ladder painting the wall. Seeing him she called out, "Hiya, Tommy, have you come to help?"

Tommy laughed. "Sure; what would you like me to do?"

Descending the ladder, she came towards him carrying a paintbrush. "Well, I would ask you to paint but, in those clothes, no way," and she laughed at her own comment.

Tommy looked down at his clothes, realising it would perhaps be better if he went home to change. "I'll just nip back to the apartment and get changed. Then I'll be right back; do you need me to bring anything?" Molly shook her head and waved as he left.

He was surprised at the progress made in renovating the place; the neighbourhood had certainly pulled together. They were well ahead of schedule, and when Marco was fully improved he would find his home intact once more. Tommy was sure, he and Carlotta would be delighted with the finished results.

Once the renovations were done the group moved on to helping Janice sort out her office and her apartment above. Fortunately, the smoke damage wasn't that severe so the job was soon finished. Within a few days, she had moved back into her place meaning peace reigned once more in Doyle's brownstone home.

* * * *

It was another six weeks before Marco and Carlotta visited Doyle at the brownstone. Marco was recovered and could move around more easily. He had insisted on visiting Tommy so he could express his sincere thanks to him for looking after Carlotta and the kids whilst he was in the hospital.

Over coffee, Tommy asked Marco how he was doing to which the man replied, "Well, another two or three weeks and I should be well enough to start sorting out the mini-market. I presume it's going to need a lot of renovation."

Tommy surprised, said, "You haven't seen the mini-market then?"

Marco shook his head. Carlotta announced, "We came straight here. We are going to check out the damage once we leave. I suppose it's very bad, Tommy?"

At that moment, the phone rang so Tommy went to answer it. He discovered Molly on the line wanting to know if it was true that Marco and Carlotta were at his place. When he confirmed they were, she suggested that he bring the couple down to the market in about ten minutes. That would give her enough time to gather as many of the people who had helped with the renovations as possible. Tommy agreed as he thought it would make a lovely surprise for the couple.

Fifteen minutes later Tommy suggested that the three of them stroll along the street to look at the market together, before going onto O'Malley's for dinner. The couple prepared themselves for the worst and leaving the brownstone the three of them slowly made their way down the street.

Turning the corner at the end of the block Doyle could see a large group of people standing outside the mini-market. Suddenly Carlotta caught sight of the group as well, pointing them out to Marco who was confused by what he saw. The closer they got to the mini-market the more amazed was the look on both the Beneto's faces.

Turning to look at Doyle, Carlotta asked, "Tommy, what is happening. I thought the market was ruined?"

Doyle smiled at her before responding, "It was, Lottie, but the folks around here didn't like the look of the place so, they decided to do a few repairs. They feel that the district just doesn't look right without the Beneto Mini Market. They did it for you, and Marco."

Standing at the entrance to the market, Marco and Carlotta could see that it looked better than before the fire. It had new windows, paintwork, doors, and a brand-new sign.

Leading the couple inside Molly took over, showing them everything that had been done. Tears streamed down the faces of Marco and Carlotta; they were astounded and amazed at the generosity of their neighbours.

"Did you know about this, Tommy," asked Marco chokingly. Doyle nodded, as Marco continued, "I don't know what to say."

Tommy leaned towards him, whispering, "Just say thank you, Marco, and tell them all how pleased you are with what they've done for you."

Marco looked at Tommy, nodded his head, then turned to the group of people, saying, "Thank you all, so very much. I cannot express how delighted I am, we are, with what you have done for us," and he trailed off into silence, overcome with emotion.

Sometime later, Tommy and the whole Beneto family were sat in O'Malley's bar celebrating the new look mini-market and, of course, Marco's return to health. There was a party atmosphere in the diner that night, so it was late when Tommy finally made it back to his apartment.

Entering the lounge, he flicked the TV set on. As the screen came to life, Columbo was just beginning his latest investigation.

'What a happy ending,' he thought, settling down to watch the great maestro once more get his man.

THE CHEATING WIFE

Doyle was sat in his office, his feet propped on top of his desk, thinking how, if anyone came into his office at that moment in time, they would conclude he was looking quite pleased with himself. For a private detective, that image wasn't too bad.

Doyle, being slightly over six feet, had strong classic features, and despite being in his early forties he still had thick black hair. He could be called a handsome man, although privately Doyle might disagree with that.

He had been sat assessing his time as a private detective. It had been nearly four years since he'd left the force and first opened his doors as a PI. In that time, he had built up a good reputation around the district. And today, he was feeling good because he realised that for the first time in many years he was attracted to a woman. The only drawback was that the object of his feelings was the local police forces ME – Dr. Veronica Martin.

A knock on the door of the office brought him back to reality. "Come in," he called, taking his feet off the desk.

The door slowly opened to reveal a slender middle-aged man with thinning hair and rimless glasses. He was Dressed in an expensive suit and carried a fedora in his hand. Hesitating, he entered the room. Doyle got up, going forward to shake the newcomer's hand.

"I'm Tommy Doyle. Please take a seat and tell me how can I help you?"

"Good afternoon, Mr. Doyle. My name is Harold James." He spoke in a low voice. "Err... you have been highly recommended as a man I can trust. You see, I have a very sensitive matter to discuss, and I've heard that you are very discreet.

Doyle told him he could trust him and asked him to explain what the problem was.

Unable to look at Doyle, the man began hesitantly. "I... err... I... suspect my wife is cheating on me but, I need to be sure. I want to know if you can find out for me? Perhaps, you could follow her when she leaves our apartment, let me know where she goes, and who she sees?"

Doyle sighed silently. Watching and following wayward husbands and wives wasn't his ideal job of being a detective. Still, it was work and put money in the bank. "Of course, I can do that, and I'll give you a full, detailed report. When would you like me to start and for how long?"

"Mmm… well, as soon as possible. And, I guess two weeks should be enough time. Unless you think you need longer?"

"No. I think two weeks will be plenty of time. My usual fees are $70 a day plus expenses.

"Yes, that's fine. Here is my card with the address. And this," he said as he passed over an envelope, "contains her picture. Oh, and err… a check for an advance payment. Please don't spare any expense."

"By the way," asked Doyle. What's your wife's name?"

"Chrissie Jayne."

Doyle held his breath for a few seconds, then slowly let it out. Chrissie Jayne James! Could it be? Doyle wondered? Could she be the same Chrissie Jayne that Mac had questioned recently regarding the disappearance of a certain young man?

If it is then this man is her husband. He opened the envelope and took out the picture and the cheque. Looking at it he couldn't say one way or the other whether it was her until he'd checked with Mac.

Mr. James stood up and, having decided Doyle's seriousness was a desire to start work on the job, he began to leave. "I see you are a man of few words. I look forward to receiving your report the next time I see you? Good day, Mr. Doyle."

"Err… yes, of course, good day, Mr. James," replied Doyle, rising from his chair to walk his new client to the door.

After James had gone, Doyle sat again at his desk. The question was, should he ring Mac, or pop into the station? After mulling it over, he picked up the phone and getting through to Mac asked him what had happened with Chrissie Jayne James' arrest.

"Why the questions, Tommy?" Mac was curious so Doyle told him about his recent visit.

"Mmm…," said Mac. "Strange one that."

"Yea it is. What do think, Mac, could the wife have been having an affair with that young man who's gone missing? Shall I take James up on his request and so some digging?"

Mac thought for a moment, before saying, "Would you mind, Tommy. Maybe you can come to the case differently from us. You up for it?"

Tommy laughed. "You trying to get me to do your job for you, Mac?"

Laughing, his pal replied, "What do you think, Tommy lad?"

Having agreed that Doyle would follow the wife for a few days, the conversation changed to the disappearance of the young man Mac had first interviewed the wayward woman about.

It seemed that following a tip-off, Mac had visited a local nightclub the victim was known to frequent, and in the course of his investigation had interviewed one Chrissie Jayne James. She had, at the time, denied any knowledge of knowing the young man, yet further inquiries had intimated that she had been seen, more than once, leaving the club at the same time as him. When questioned about this, the lady had insisted it was pure co-incidence them leaving at the same time.

As Mac couldn't prove any different, he had left it. But something had niggled him about the woman's insistence that she didn't know the young man, and her being a happily married woman to a wealthy man. After all, what happily married woman spent her free time in a back street club?

Over the next few days, Doyle did as Mr. James had requested. Each morning, he waited until Chrissie James left the house, then he followed her.

The first two or three days she went shopping, to the hairdresser, or had coffee with friends. Each afternoon she spent at the local spa. Whether she met anyone inside Doyle couldn't determine, as there were some places even he couldn't enter. Either way, she had returned home in time to greet Mr. James on the doorstep as he pulled his car into the Driveway.

Doyle was feeling frustrated. But, not for long.

On the fourth day, not long after Mr. James had left for the office, a limousine pulled up outside the James resident. Two minutes later, Chrissie James left the house and climbed into the back of the car. As it drove away, Doyle jumped into his vehicle and followed at a safe distance.

As it happened, he recognised whose car it was. Only one man owned a limo that looked like that – and that was Jo Jo Grimondi – Doyle and Mac's favourite gangster Don.

'Well, well, well,' thought Doyle. He knew Mac would be interested in this development, but he would have to wait to hear about it.

The limo car sped across the city until finally, it pulled up at one of the poshest restaurants in town. Luigi's. Leaving the car Chrissie went inside.

Parking up, Doyle nipped to the phone booth and rang Mac, telling him the latest news. Then, going around the back of the restaurant he nipped in the back door, nodding to Roberto the head waiter.

"Signor Doyle, how are you?"

"Very well, Roberto. Can I have a peek into the dining room?"

Roberto looked surprised, but said, "OK. You on a job?"

Doyle nodded his head. Then carefully opening the door a little, he searched the room until he spotted Jo Jo. Sat next to him was Chrissie Jayne, being all lovey-dovey with Jo Jo.

'Mmm…" thought Doyle, 'So that's the game. Mmm…'

Fifteen minutes later, Mac, walked into the kitchen. "Hey, Tommy. I'm off around the front to talk to Jo Jo, you want to join me?"

About to say yes, Doyle changed his mind. "No, might be better if Mrs. James, doesn't meet me just yet? Don't want to blow my cover?"

Mac nodded and left the kitchen.

Quickly climbing into his car he drove round to the front of the restaurant, where he parked up before entering the building and heading straight towards Jo Jo's table. Doyle watched from the doorway into the kitchen.

"Afternoon, Jo Jo. How's things?" said Mac.

Jo Jo Grimondi looked up as one of his henchmen stepped forward to stop Mac from approaching the table. Mac waved his badge under the man's face, snarling at him to back off.

Jo Jo waved his hand and the guy reluctantly stepped back. "And what can I do for you, Inspector Mackintosh? Can't you see I'm entertaining a lady?"

Mac laughed. "Oh! I can see Jo Jo. Mind you, I somehow think this particular lady's husband might not approve of the company she's keeping. What say you, Mrs. James?"

"I say it's none of your business who I have lunch with, Inspector," said Chrissie James, a smirk crossing her face. "And I don't think my husband will be too bothered, either way."

Mac looked at her for a few moments. Then leaning a little closer he whispered, "Oh, I wouldn't bet on that Mrs. James. Divorce can be a very messy business when the wife gets caught out playing away from home," and Mac smiled to take the sting out of his words.

Straightening he turned ready to leave, then stopping, he turned back. "By the way Jo Jo, did you know a young man by the name of Edward Brown?"

Jo Jo looked Mac in the eyes, replying, "Never heard of him."

"I hope that's the truth Jo Jo. I wouldn't like to be in your shoes if I find out you've been lying to me.

106

Enjoy your lunch, Mrs. James, Jo Jo," and Mac left the restaurant.

Ten minutes later Mac and Doyle met in a local coffee shop part way down the street. They sat in the window where they had a good view of the doorway of the fancy restaurant Jo-Jo and Chrissie James were having lunch in.

"What do you think, Tommy?"

"Mmm... not too sure. If she's Jo Jo's new bit of stuff then maybe he got rid of the lad? It's got me stumped at the moment. Maybe I should pay Mrs. James a visit and see what I can get out of her?" suggested Doyle.

Mac agreed, telling Doyle to be careful and that he would catch up with him later at O' Malley's bar. Parting company they went their separate ways.

Two hours later the black limo dropped Chrissie James off at her home. Doyle was waiting. As soon as the limo had gone, he got out of his car and went to ring the doorbell of the house. When the door opened Chrissie James was stood there Dressed in a delicate housecoat of silk and lace.

"Yes? Can I help you?" she asked.

Flashing his PI identity, he introduced himself and asked if she could spare him some time to answer a few questions.

Looking Doyle up and down, she thought, 'Here was a good-looking man.' One she could be interested in. Doyle recognised that look. It wasn't the first time he had seen it.

She spoke in a soft sultry voice. "What about, Mr.… err… Doyle?" she said as she looked at his ID. "Why don't you come inside?"

Following her into the house, Doyle noticed the sight and smell of wealth. He was interested in the way Chrissie James sashayed down the hall as she led him into the drawing-room. It was a walk meant to turn a man on. She knew exactly what she was doing. Unfortunately for her, she was not Doyle's type, so the effect was, in the main, lost on him. Still, he found her attempts amusing.

"Please, Mr. Doyle, won't you sit and tell me what it is you want to know," asked Chrissie as she sat, ensuring her housecoat slipped open slightly at the front to reveal her silicone-enhanced breasts and her long slender legs.

On any other man the effect could have been a turn-on, but again not for Doyle. He had seen too many such women plying their trades on the streets to be turned on by some second-rate married woman who dated a gangster Don.

"I am investigating a missing person. The family of a young man called Edward Brown has asked me to try and trace him. I have been led to believe that you might have known the young man. Perhaps met him at a club called... The Thunder Dome?"

Doyle did his best to make the question sound innocent, before continuing with. "You might only have seen him in passing, but I am trying to gather as much information as possible about his movements on the night of 16th last."

Chrissie pulled the housecoat tightly around her. "I don't think I know this young man."

"Well, it's not so much that you might know him, Mrs... err..."

"James, Chrissie James."

"Mrs. James. It's just that as you were at the club on the night of the 16th, I did wonder if perhaps you might have seen the young man talking to anyone in particular, or leaving with somebody? Can I show you a picture?" and Doyle pulled a photo of Edward Brown from his pocket to show her.

With a slight shake of her hand, Chrissie took the photo and looked at it. Then she quickly proffered it back to Doyle. "No, sorry. I don't recognise him."

Doyle didn't take the photo, but looked at Chrissie and said, "Please, Mrs. James. Will you look again, just to be sure? He has a young sister of ten years old, well step-sister really but they were very close and she has been crying because he missed her birthday. And he's never missed her birthday. So, please have another look and see if you can remember him. Or just anything about him or someone he might have been talking to that night?"

Chrissie swallowed and re-looked at the photo. After a few seconds, she handed the photo back. This time Doyle took it.

"All, I can remember is that Edward, that's what you called him right? Well, the young man, got into an argument with someone. I'm not sure what it was about, but the other guy wasn't very nice. I think he followed Edward, the young man, outside and… and… I'm sorry that's all I remember. I wasn't that close to them so I didn't take much notice," and her voice trailed off.

Doyle knew he had gotten all he could, for now, so rising he thanked her and said if she thought of anything else would she contact him or the police. At the mention of the police, Chrissie looked terrified. Doyle offered her his card and saying goodbye, he left.

After Doyle had gone Chrissie James wasn't sure what to do. She knew she couldn't say anything, not even to her husband. And especially not to Jo Jo. What the hell had she gone and got herself into? She needed to think but now was not the time. Edmund would be home soon so she had better go get dressed. She would think about Doyle's visit later.

* * * *

Two days later, as Doyle was making coffee, there was a knock at his office door. "Come," he yelled.

The door slowly opened and in walked Chrissie James. "Mr. Doyle? I don't know if you remember me?"

Doyle smiled. "Mrs. James! Come in. Want a coffee? Sorry, no milk. But I got sugar."

Smiling back, Chrissie said, "Thanks, but no sugar. I need it strong and black this morning."

"Take a seat, Chrissie. I can call you Chrissie, can't I?"

"Yes, Tommy. You can," and relaxing she sat down.

Doyle passed her a mug of coffee and sitting down himself he asked, "So, Chrissie, what can I do for you?"

Taking a sip of the strong hot brew to give her courage, Chrissie James, finally spoke. "I'm in trouble, Mr. Doyle. It's my own stupid fault, I know. I've got involved with the wrong type of person and I don't know how to get out of the situation. If you think you can help, I would be eternally grateful," and shaking slightly, she took a few more sips of the coffee to help settle her nerves.

Doyle didn't speak for a moment or two, causing Chrissie to wonder why. She was just about to ask, when he said, "Jo Jo Grimondi. Is he your situation, Chrissie?" She nodded, looking surprised that Doyle had guessed.

"You know Chrissie, it would help if you told me everything; start at the beginning."

Looking Doyle in the eyes, Chrissie realised that if she was going to escape the mess she was in, then she had to trust this man. Taking a deep breath, she began talking; telling him all that had happened to her over the last few months. By the time she had finished speaking Chrissie felt drained, yet liberated that she had bared her soul.

For a moment Doyle didn't say anything. Then he told her, "Chrissie, you need to tell the police what you have told me. I know it's not going to be easy. That it's going to be scary, but if I promise to stay by your side until it's all over, will you do what I ask?"

Swallowing hard, Chrissie looked scared as she whispered, "They'll kill me…"

"No, no, Chrissie, they won't. Because I won't let that happen to you. I promise."

Looking Doyle in the face, she saw the sincerity in his eyes and decided that could she trust him. Nodding her head, she whispered, "Okay, Mr. Doyle, what happens next?"

"Well, I'll get my pal Mac, Inspector Pete Mackintosh to come over and take a statement from you. Then we'll arrange for you to stay somewhere safe while Mac investigates. Perhaps your husband can help us?"

"I'm not sure," she said uncertainly. "Once he hears what's happened, he'll probably divorce me. Looks like I'll be going from one bad situation to another," and she laughed a little hysterically.

Doyle thought for a moment, then said, "I wonder, Chrissie? Maybe your husband might surprise you. Let's see what happens, shall we?"

An hour later, Mac arrived at Doyle's brownstone building to learn more from Chrissie, and to take a statement. What he heard surprised him, and left him knowing her testimony would blow the case wide open on the missing young man Edward Brown. Fortunately, like Doyle, Mac was able to ease

Chrissie's mind, meaning she managed to give her statement without too much problem.

Once she had finished speaking, Mac said, "Mrs. James, I want to thank you for co-operating and telling me everything. You don't know what this will mean to the Brown family. If we can find out what happened to their son it will give the family peace. I also want you to know that we, Tommy and I will look after you. We'll make sure you are kept safe, this I promise."

Feeling reassured, Doyle asked her if she would like to pop upstairs and refresh herself while he and Mac finished chatting. Then he would sort out what was to happen next. Nodding Chrissie left the office.

After she'd gone, Mac said, "So, Tommy, what d'ya think?"

Tommy sighed. "Well, Mac, if you can make it stick it will be a big feather in your cap. It will mean keeping her, and her old man safe, until the trial though, won't it?"

Mac nodded his head. "Yea, that's the thing, Tommy. Any suggestions?"

Laughing, Tommy said, "I sometimes think you think I'm daft. I know what you're wanting, so come on spit it out!"

Mac smiled, "Never could pull the wool over your eyes, Tommy lad. Okay, how about some protection duty? Keep the rich lady company? You up for it?"

"If it helps, then count me in."

"That's great, Tommy. I knew I could rely on you. Now, how do we approach the husband?"

"Why don't you leave him to me, Mac?" His pal nodded in agreement; after all, Edmund James was Tommy's client.

After Mac had left, Chrissie rejoined Tommy in his office. "Mr. Doyle, what do you suggest I do?"

"Well, Chrissie, the first thing we are going to do is go and chat with your husband."

"What! No!" she gasped. "He'll kill me. I can't…" and her voice trailed off into a whisper.

Holding his hand up to calm her down, Tommy began telling her what he would say to Chrissie's husband. Looking up in surprise, a smile slowly crossed her face. "Really… Mr. Doyle? You'll tell him all that?"

"Yes, I will," and he smiled at her. "But you have to back me up, okay?"

Chrissie nodded her head, suddenly realising that maybe, just maybe, things would turn out alright. She would keep her fingers crossed."

An hour later, Doyle and Chrissie arrived at the James' residence, being met at the door by Mr. James who was worried about his missing wife. He was also surprised to see Doyle with his wife. However, before he could say anything Tommy introduced himself.

"Good afternoon, Mr. James. My name is Tommy Doyle, I'm a Private Investigator but I work with the local police precinct in the fourth district. I don't want to worry you but is it possible that I could come in and explain what has happened?"

Whilst James was of course surprised, he took his lead from Doyle. "Of... of course, please come in. Are you okay, Chrissie darling?"

"Yes, Edmund I am fine, really," she replied, smiling.

Following Mr. James into the drawing-room, Doyle sat, declining the offer of a drink. Once everyone was settled, he began explaining. "Mr. James, it appears that Mrs. James, unbeknownst to her, is a material witness in a missing person case."

"What! How?" cried James.

"Now, don't panic," said Doyle quickly. "However, Chrissie, err... Mrs. James will have to give testimony against the perpetrators. Which means she will have to attend a line-up and a court case, but..." and here Doyle paused, "I don't want you to worry as we, the police and I, are going to do all we can to protect her."

"No! She can't. Not if it puts her in danger," said Mr. James, stunned. "Chrissie, say you can't, no you won't do it?"

Chrissie looked at Doyle, who sat waiting to see if her positive strength of earlier would leave her in the presence of her husband's demands.

Seeing Doyle waiting for her to agree with Edmund, she knew that if she did, she would never be free of the mess she was in. It was now or never. Somehow the look on Tommy Doyle's face reassured her that he would make sure she would be safe.

Straightening her back, Chrissie took a deep breath, and looking her husband in her eyes, she replied, "No, Edmund. I will not refuse to do the right thing. No matter how painful it is going to be, I am going to testify. There is a young child who is missing her brother. I will not be held responsible for that child not knowing what has happened to him.

Chrissie paused and looked at Doyle once again. "I trust Mr. Doyle, and if he says I will be protected, then I believe him. Edmund. you can either support me or not. The decision is yours," and at that point, she stood up and looking at Doyle, she asked, "Should I pack a large or small suitcase, Tommy?"

Doyle swallowed hard, doing his best to hide a smile. "Make it a large suitcase, as I'm not sure how long you'll be under police protection."

Nodding her head, Chrissie bent towards her husband and kissing him on his forehead she said, "I'm sorry, Edmund. I have to do the right thing," then turning she left the room. Edmund watched her leave, his mouth opened in surprise.

After she had gone, he turned towards Doyle, asking, "What the hell, Doyle, I asked you to follow my wife, not get her involved in some criminal case. What are you playing at?"

Doyle coughed. "Mr. James, I did not get your wife involved in anything. It was by sheer accident that she came up in the police files as a witness. I just happen to know the police officer handling the case. We work together and he has asked me to assist him."

"Oh! I see. Err... what about the other matter," Edmund, whispered, all the while surreptitiously watching the room door in case his wife returned.

Doyle took a moment to swallow and silently pray to the PI's God for forgiveness for the lie he was about to make, before responding. "Well, Mr. James, as far as that's concerned, there's nothing much to report. Your wife did all the usual things the wife of a wealthy man would do. She visited the shops, no doubt spending your hard-earned money. Also went to the spa a couple of times a week, and had coffee with other similar wives. The only bad thing I would say she did, if it can be classed as bad, was to visit a rather un-impressive club a couple of times, no doubt enticed on by some of her friends. It was during one of these visits that she became an unwitting witness to the possible disappearance of a young man. That's it."

"That's it?" asked Edmund, totally surprised at Doyle's report. If he was honest, he really had thought his wife had been playing away from home. But if Doyle said not, well then he was obviously wrong. And after all, Doyle had come highly recommended.

So, Mr. Doyle, what happens next?"

Relieved that James had accepted his version of things, Doyle swallowed before replying, "I am going to place your wife somewhere safe. I cannot tell you where it is, as it leaves you vulnerable. In fact… if I could suggest something?"

"Anything, Mr. Doyle, anything. All I want is for Chrissie to be safe."

"Is there somewhere you could go and stay for a few weeks? Somewhere private? That way the police won't have to worry about you, as well as Chrissie."

James thought about what Doyle was suggesting. He knew the PI was right. Whoever was involved in this young man's disappearance could well want Chrissie to disappear as well. And one way to get at her was through him. Finally, he said, "Yes, Mr. Doyle, there is somewhere I can go. When should I leave?"

"Leave! Who is leaving?" asked a shocked Chrissie James, as she entered the room.

As both men stood up, Doyle told Chrissie that it would be best if Edmund left the house and went away until after the trial. It meant he would be safe, but more importantly, so would she. Relieved that her husband wasn't intending to leave her for good, Chrissie, of course, could see the sense in Doyle's suggestion.

"I see, Mr. Doyle. Yes, yes, that's a good suggestion, Edmund. If anything happened to you, I could never live with myself."

Seeing the sincerity in his wife's eyes, James stood, took her in his arms, and kissed her tenderly, whispering, "How could I have doubted you?"

For a moment, Doyle was slightly embarrassed, but it dawned on him, that despite her flirtation with Jo Jo Grimondi, Chrissie James did, in fact, love her husband deeply. Shaking his head slightly, Doyle realised he would never understand women.

"Okay, guys," started Doyle, "we need to get moving. I have arranged for a police presence to be placed outside your house for the next few days until you manage to arrange a place to stay. Okay, Mrs. James?"

Mr. James nodded in agreement. "Is that necessary? Of course, it is, Mr. Doyle. That was a stupid question, wasn't it? So, what next?"

Relaxing, Doyle sat the pair down and slowly explained what was going to happen. By the time he had finished, he knew both Edmund and Chrissie understood the importance of following his instructions to the letter. With the suggestion that Mr. James finds somewhere else to go to live, Edmund went into his office to make the necessary arrangements.

After Edmund had left the room, Doyle and Chrissie sat in silence for short while. Finally, she spoke, "I want to thank you, Mr. Doyle. If I am honest, I wasn't sure Edmund would believe you."

Putting his fingers to his lips to shush her, Doyle replied, "No problem, Chrissie. All I ask is that you trust me and do as I ask. It's for your safety. Okay?"

Nodding her head, Chrissie, smiled. "Anything you say, Mr. Doyle."

An hour later, with all the arrangements made for Mr. James's departure, the couple said their goodbyes. Doyle, finally interrupting their parting embrace by saying, "Now, remember, no communication with each other. When you arrive at your destination, Edmund, I want you to purchase a new phone. Don't sign a contract, just go for a pay-as-you-go sim. You can ring me on this number," and Doyle passed him a piece of paper.

Continuing he said, "You will let the phone ring three times, then you will hang up. Wait for two minutes, then ring again. I will answer. If I don't answer, don't worry. It probably means I am not available. Leave it. Do NOT try again for at least half an hour. I may ring you back. BUT I will do the same. I will let the phone ring three times, hang up, and then retry. All the instructions are on that paper. Do you understand?"

Edmund looked at the paper, before nodding his head that he understood. "Will I be able to speak to Chrissie?"

"If she's with me, then yes. If not, I will arrange for her to ring you. However, you must not use your normal mobiles, so I want you to give them to me now, please?"

Reluctantly, the James's handed over their mobile phones. "Is that them all," Doyle asked seriously. Both said yes. Despite their replies, Doyle wasn't sure Chrissie was being honest about it, but he let it go for now.

"Edmund, you will NOT under any circumstances tell anyone, and I mean anyone, where you are. To do so means I cannot guarantee your safety, and it will put Chrissie's life in danger. Do you understand me?"

Mr. James nodded his head, but didn't answer, nor did he look Doyle in the eyes.

At that moment the doorbell rang. Going to the window, Doyle peeked through the net curtains. Stood at the front door were a couple of police officers. As they turned towards him, Doyle recognised Smithy and Craig; two good cops who worked for Mac. Leaving the room, he quickly let the pair into the house and explained the current situation before taking them into the room to meet the James couple.

"Mr. James, this is Smithy and Craig, they are going to stay here until you are ready to leave. I have brought them up to speed on your plans, so they will escort you to the airport and ensure you leave the city safely. They are good cops and can be trusted, so please follow their instructions, they won't steer you wrong."

The doorbell rang again. Smithy checked through the window. "It's Mac, Tommy, shall I let him in?" Doyle nodded his head.

As Mac entered the room, he was introduced to Edmund, shaking his hand, before asking if everything was set up. "Sure is, Mac," Doyle told him. "Chrissie is packed, and Edmund is all set for his departure."

"I just need to go and pack, Inspector."

Mac acknowledged Mr. James' comment and suggested he go do it now. After he had left the room, Doyle looked at Chrissie, saying, "Okay, Chrissie, time to go. Come on," then taking her gently but firmly by the arm they left the room.

Smithy and Craig checked outside to make sure the coast was clear as Doyle packed Chrissie's luggage in the boot of his car, before escorting her to the front seat. Climbing into the driver's side, he thanked the two cops, saluted Mac. "See you later." He then drove away.

"Where are we going, Tommy?"

Concentrating on the road, as well as making sure he wasn't being followed, Doyle didn't answer straight away. Finally, he told her, "For now you are going to stay at my place. There is a spare apartment on the top floor. You should be safe there. My security is second to none. However, if I need to move you, I have another place lined up."

Chrissie didn't say anything. Not much she could say really.

Doyle took her silence for fear. Glancing at her, he said, "Don't worry, Chrissie. I told you I would look after you, and I will. I always keep my word, honest!"

Turning to look at him, she smiled. She believed him. Tommy Doyle was a man you could trust.

Doyle decided to Drive the long way back to the brownstone, just in case he was being followed. You never knew. After all, he wasn't getting any younger, and a recent case had brought home to him that his powers of observation in not being spotted when on a job could well have diminished. (The Severino stakeout jumped immediately to mind.)

As it turned out, Doyle wasn't followed and they arrived back at the brownstone with no problem.

Driving into the underground garage, Doyle secured the doors before leaving the car. Once he was happy everything was secure, he helped Chrissie out. Then taking her luggage, they went up in the secret lift he had installed inside the old chimney of the building. Doyle could have had the lift made available for everyone to use, but he felt walking up the stairs helped keep him fit and healthy. And he was certain that was good, especially for a man of his age.

Settling Chrissie in the spare apartment, Doyle was about to leave when Chrissie said, "Mr. Doyle, I owe you an apology."

Stopping he turned to look, seeing her standing and holding out a cell phone. "I didn't want to give you this in front of Edmund, as he would have wanted to know why I had it. I am so sorry. Forgive me, please."

Doyle smiled. Taking the phone, he said, "I did wonder, Chrissie, as I didn't think you would communicate with Jo Jo on your regular phone. Is it switched off?"

Chrissie nodded yes. "Shall I turn it on?"

"No. Is there a password?" Chrissie gave him the password. "Better not turn it on in here, just in case they try to trace it. I'll give it to Mac. He'll know what to do with it. Thanks, Chrissie. Is there anything else you haven't told me?"

For a moment Chrissie hesitated. She appeared reluctant to speak. "Anything?" said Doyle. "Remember you have to be honest and trust me."

"You know, I got the feeling you were following me. If I am honest, I hoped you were and that you would tell Edmund that I was having an affair."

Doyle was surprised, asking, "Why?"

"Because I believed that Edmund was being unfaithful to me. I thought if I did it back, he would get jealous and realise what a fool he was, and stop seeing whoever it was he was meeting. I'm sorry I should have told you before, shouldn't I?"

"Mmm… well, I'm not sure it would have made any difference to the case, but it might to you and what happens later. Thanks for telling me. Now get yourself settled in. I'm going to make us something to eat. I'll call you when it's ready. By the way, I'm across the hall," and Doyle turned to leave.

Stopping in the doorway, he turned and said, "You were right, Chrissie. I was following you. Edmund asked me to find out if you were having an affair. When I told him you weren't I wasn't sure if he was surprised or disappointed? Oh well, that's something to sort out later. Don't worry about it for now. Get settled." And on that note, Doyle left the room.

He had a lot to think about. One thing he had been right about was Edmund James's reaction. He had appeared disappointed when Doyle had told him Chrissie hadn't been cheating on him. It was almost as if he knew she was having an affair and wanted her to be caught out? Was the man being two-faced? Had he pulled the wool over Doyle's eyes and was actually cheating himself? Mmm... this was a quandary. No wonder James had been reluctant to go away.

'I think I need to dig deeper into Mr. James's life,' thought Tommy as he entered his apartment. Yes, he would need to look a little deeper.

* * * *

Over the next couple of weeks, Chrissie settled into the brownstone with little effort. She missed going out and not being in communication with her friends, but overall, she was feeling at peace with herself. Jo Jo Grimondi had been a mistake, a very bad mistake. She had known that at the time but he had been so charming – deadly – but charming.

However, when compared to someone like Tommy Doyle, Chrissie could see where she'd gone wrong. Now there was a man she could have had a real affair with. She began to wonder if he found her attractive? If she could she turn him on? With nothing much to fill her mind, Chrissie began to wonder what it would be like to be kissed by the tall, dark-haired, athletic, older man that Doyle was. She also began to wonder if he was any good in bed. Perhaps, she should find out?

Unfortunately, despite being a good-looking woman, and even Doyle would admit desirable, him bedding Chrissie James was not part of the job. Therefore the lady was to find herself disappointed in her expectations.

To allow Chrissie to go out occasionally, Doyle arranged for the local hairdresser to come and fit her with a couple of wigs. The difference this made to Chrissie's appearance was amazing, especially when glasses were added and she stopped wearing the heavy make-up she normally wore. With a couple of new outfits that were not the style normally worn by her, Chrissie soon became Teresa Jones, Doyle's cousin from Bakersfield, Mid-California. It was surprising how good the disguises turned out to be.

However, Doyle insisted that Chrissie should not venture out unless he was with her, as a contract had been put out on her. When Chrissie heard this, she almost collapsed with shock. Settling her down, Tommy told her not to worry, she was perfectly safe with him and it would soon all be over.

* * * *

A week later, Mac approached Tommy's brownstone home. Before entering he bent to tie his shoe-lace, taking the opportunity to search the area. Closing the door behind him, Mac looked up at the camera and signalled for Tommy to lock the front door. Shortly afterward he heard the click of the automatic dead bolts click into place. Heading for the staircase, Doyle met his pal as he hit the first-floor landing, ushering him into his office.

"What's up, Mac?"

Checking the streets below through the office window, Mac said, "I think we've been nobbled. I'm sure I caught sight of one of Grimondi's henchmen out on the street. Yea, there he is," and he pointed to a guy trying to be inconspicuous but not doing a very good job of it.

Checking through the other window, Doyle said, "Damn, how the hell did they guess where she was? We've been so careful. Not told a soul. Mmm…" Doyle was not happy.

The door to the office opened. "Is something wrong, Mr. Doyle?" It was Chrissie James.

Doyle and Mac looked at each other. "Can I ask you, Chrissie? Have you by any chance told anyone, at all, where you have been staying?" asked Mac.

Chrissie looked surprised. "Me? No, Inspector, Tommy was quite clear that I mustn't tell any… one… only…" and she stopped speaking as her voice trailed away.

"What is it, Chrissie? Did you say something to someone?" asked Doyle. "If you did, we need to know, now."

"I… but he wouldn't… would he…" and she started to cry, as something dawned on her that left the two men stumped.

"Okay, okay, Chrissie, tell me what it is. Who did you tell?" asked Doyle gently. "If it's a mistake I'm not going to yell, honest."

Looking up at him, tears rolling down her face, Chrissie finally whispered, "Edmund. I told Edmund… He asked me where I was and without thinking I told him. But I swore him to secrecy,

131

honestly I did. And he promised not to tell anyone. He wouldn't tell..." and she started crying even more.

Doyle looked at Mac, who mouthed 'The husband?' Tommy nodded yes.

"Right, Chrissie, I want you to do me a favour, okay?" asked Mac.

"Anything, Inspector. Just tell me."

"Right, we need to get you to safety. So, what I'm going to do is arrange for a woman police officer to take your place. She'll need to dress in your clothes and borrow one of the wigs. I'll need to know what size you are?" asked Mac.

Having got the details, Mac rang the precinct and told Clarky what had happened and to organise a female cop to swap places with Chrissie. Whoever they got had to be trusted, and had to fill the measurements given by Chrissie. With a few other instructions, a plan was put into action.

"Now, Chrissie, I want you to ring your husband?" said Mac.

"Do I have to? If he's the one who told them I don't want to speak to him ever again, the bastard."

Doyle laughed, "Now that's the attitude we want, Chrissie. I think what Mac wants you to do is to tell your husband, secretly of course, that you are being moved to another secret location. You are going to have to make it sound good, Chrissie. Do you think you can do that?"

Chrissie was realising that Edmund wasn't all she thought he was. Thinking about it some more, she decided she would do anything to show him up. But, he wasn't going to get away with hurting her. She would show him. "Okay, Inspector, Tommy. You tell me exactly what you want me to say and I'll do it."

Half an hour later, following the instructions she had been given, Chrissie Jayne James put on the best performance of her life. As she did, Doyle sat listening.

"Oh, Edmund, I do miss you so much." Pause while she listens. "Yes, I know. But it won't be too long. You do love me don't you, Edmund?" Another pause as she listened to his response, one which made her screw up her lips in anger. Calming herself, she carried on.

"Well, I'd better go, before Mr. Doyle captures me talking to you. Oh, by the way, Edmund. I forgot to tell you they are moving me, tomorrow. Yes. Moving me. I think the Inspector said something about early in the morning. At sunrise. You know, how bad I am getting up so early so I hope it's not true. No, Edmund. He said tomorrow. As soon as I know where I am I will ring you and let you know. Oh! I think that sounds like Mr. Doyle coming. I love you, Edmund. I can't wait for us to be together again. Bye, darling," and she finished the call.

Silence reigned for a few minutes. Then Chrissie burst into tears. "How could he do this to me? Why?"

Taking her in his arms, Doyle didn't say anything. He just let Chrissie cry herself out.

Eventually, the tears ceased, and looking up at Doyle, Chrissie, whispered, "Thank you, Tommy. That was very kind of you."

As he looked at her, Doyle was suddenly tempted to bend his head and kiss her. And he would have, had he not heard Mac and the poker night boys coming up the stairs. The moment passed with some regret on both sides.

"How did the call go, Tommy?" Mac asked as he entered the room.

"Fine. Chrissie sure was convincing. Although she cracked up afterward. Sobbed her heart out. Think it's finally hit her that Edmund isn't all he's led her to believe he is."

"Mmm… Makes me think he set her up, somehow?"

Doyle wasn't sure but he agreed with Mac. "Okay, Mac. What's the plan?"

That night the boys from the precinct held their usual Tuesday Poker night. They were joined by a couple of woman officers, who also liked playing Poker.

Chrissie, having calmed down and shed her tears, also joined them. She proved to be a formidable player, meaning the game went on until the early hours of the morning, or at least that is what the Grimondi henchmen stationed outside were led to believe. It was a cold night, and rained heavily, whilst inside the boys and girls in blue spent the night either keeping watch on the outside or sleeping.

As dawn surfaced, the two woman cops left in one of the other guy's cars which had been parked in Doyle's underground garage. As they left a police van rolled in.

Half an hour later the van left. Inside were Mac, three armed police officers, and a young woman in an auburn wig, blue suit, and hat, with dark glasses partly covering her face. Just as it turned the corner of the back street, two black sedans followed at a safe distance.

As the police van left the area, Mac and the officers sat inside prepared themselves ready for an attack. It didn't happen until they were outside the city limits, crossing Mulholland Highway, heading

North. Unfortunately, for the attackers, they omitted to spot the eye-in-the-sky chopper, which had been following them from the moment the van left Doyle's place.

Finally, the two cars moved in, but the unexpected happened. Mac was ready for them. Stopping the van, the cops inside threw open all the doors and bounced out, guns blazing. The villains didn't stand a chance.

And when they tried to drive away, the chopper flew down and dropped white powder over the windscreen. Not being able to see soon found the cars dumped in the ditch running up the side of the road.

Surrounded by police who weren't afraid to open fire, saw the villains laying down their weapons and surrendering. Mac was happy and the bad guys were left wondering how they were going to explain this to their boss, Jo Jo Grimondi.

Fifteen minutes after the police van had left the garage, Doyle had left in his car heading for the fourth precinct.

Once there, he collected one of the woman police officers, then he had quickly driven out of town.

* * * *

An hour later, having ensured he wasn't being followed, Doyle drove into a private residence in the Twin Peaks area. Checking the area was clear, the pair left the car, making their way towards the large sprawling house.

Entering the building, the young woman looked around. "Wow, Mr. Doyle, this is marvellous. Who does it belong to?"

Doyle looked around, and then at Chrissie James who was dressed as a police officer. Smiling, he simply said, "Me," before turning to go and fetch the small suitcase and the box of groceries stashed in the boot of his car.

Chrissie James wandered around the house, exploring each room with delight. She was amazed that Doyle owned such a place.

Doyle put the car in the garage, again double-checking that the area was clear of strangers. As he was about to return to the house a police car pulled up. "Afternoon, Inspector Doyle.

Doyle turned to greet the young officer leaning out of the car window. "Afternoon, Ted. How are you doing?"

"Not bad, Sir. You on holiday, or is it another job?"

"It's a job, Ted. I'll be here for a couple of days only. Okay?"

"Yes, Sir, no problem. I'll keep my eyes peeled. Give me a ring if you need help. Numbers the same. Have a good evening."

"Thanks, Ted. Oh! By the way Ted, less of the Sir, I'm not an Inspector anymore, remember? Although on this job, I am working with Mac. Have a good night, Ted."

Entering the house, Doyle locked the front door, again double-checking the area. He did it through force of habit more than anything else. It was nice the local cops still showed him respect. It meant they could work well together, when necessary.

"Friend or foe, Mr. Doyle," Chrissie James asked.

Doyle laughed. "Friend. A good one too. So, have you made yourself at home then?"

"Yes. Now, why don't you go and have a shower, while I make you something to eat. I promise not to burn the place down," and Chrissie laughed.

Doyle liked the sound.

As he went for a shower, he called out, "Remember, don't open the door, Chrissie. To anyone, okay?"

Promising she wouldn't, Chrissie went into the kitchen. For the first time in the weeks, since all this nonsense had started, she felt relaxed and at peace with the world. And it was all thanks to Tommy Doyle.

A couple of hours later, after a lovely meal of Mustard Glazed Salmon, with Rice and Green Veg, Doyle and Chrissie sat in front of the open fire, lights low, relaxing. Doyle's eyes were closed as he enjoyed the peaceful atmosphere.

"Tommy," whispered Chrissie, as she sat down on the sofa next to him.

"Mmm…" said Tommy, thinking it best not to open his eyes and look at her.

"I wanted to say, thank you. For saving my life and for looking after me so well."

Doyle didn't respond immediately, as he was absorbing the smell of her perfume. "No worries, Chrissie. It's all part of the job."

"I know, Tommy. But, I was brought up to say thank you when someone did something good for you," and she snuggled up close to him.

The warmth of her, the smell of not just her perfume but of her whole being was becoming over-powering. He only had to turn his head, and he could kiss her. He could. But he shouldn't.

'Why not?' he thought. 'She obviously wants me to.' He knew he needed to move or else who knew what would happen.

"Tommy."

"Yes," he whispered.

"Are you going to kiss me, or not?"

And there it was. The invitation he needed, wanted. Slowly opening his eyes, he turned his head and looked down at her. She was staring at him. Her mouth was slightly open, ready to be taken. Without stopping to think of the consequences Tommy bent his head and slowly their lips met.

To Doyle it was wonderful. Something he hadn't done in a long time. Awakening a feeling he had long since forgotten. The kiss grew deeper and before he knew it, he was on top of her, caressing her so perfect body. Starting to undress her his desire was growing.

Hell, this was all wrong but suddenly he wanted her. His hand slipped inside her blouse to feel her firm breasts, arousing him, making him hard.

Things were progressing fast, and as she whispered, "Take me, Tommy, take me," a loud knocking sounded at the front door.

Within seconds, Doyle was off the sofa demanding, "Quick, go hide in the cupboard under the stairs."

Seeing the seriousness of his face, Chrissie didn't need telling twice. She was off the settee and running.

Doyle, collected his gun, and approaching the front door, he called out, "Who is it?"

"It's me, Mac. Come on Doyle, open the bloody door, it's cold and wet out here."

Breathing a sigh of relief, not just for it being Mac, but also because he was saved from being caught in an embarrassing situation, Doyle quickly opened the door. "You gave me quite a start, Mac. What the hell is wrong. Come on in."

Mac walked into the house, looking around. "You took your time answering. Where's Chrissie?"

"She's in the cupboard under the stairs. We were both snoozing in front of the fire," explained Tommy. "What's up. I thought you we weren't going to talk until trial."

"Ahh… Tommy," said Mac. "Well, that's why I'm here. So, there you are Chrissie. Do you like Doyle's cupboard?" and he laughed.

Chrissie laughed nervously. "Not really. You scared me."

"Sorry. Should have warned you I was on my way."

"Okay, Mac, spill," said Doyle.

Grabbing a glass of wine, Mac sat down and began his tale. It appeared, that following the surrender of the henchmen who had tried to ambush the police van, Mac had managed to get a couple of them to talk. They were relatively new to the Grimondi family, so hadn't yet learnt not to open their mouths. What they told Mac led him to discover the body of Edward Brown. They also managed to point the finger at the two guys who had made Brown disappear; one of whom Chrissie had already identified.

"Anyway, to cut a long story short, I paid our friendly Don a personal visit. And this time I went with a good warrant. Stripped his house bare. Fortunately, his sisters weren't home. Do you know, Tommy, it's surprising what you can find inside a gangsters' safe, especially when they don't want you to. The old man would be furious if he knew how sloppy Jo Jo has been with his paperwork," and Mac laughed.

"Do you mean you got him?" asked Tommy.

"Sure did. And, depending on your point of view, I also got Edmund James for conspiracy to commit attempted murder."

"What! What do you mean, you got Edmund? Whose murder?" asked a shocked Chrissie.

Mac looked at Doyle before answering. "Yours, Chrissie. He had you lined up to be topped. The only problem was, Jo Jo, fancied you so he thought he'd have a bit of fun first. And that's the only reason you've lived as long as you have."

Suddenly Chrissie ran from the room. In the bathroom, she threw up the tasty meal she had prepared. 'It can't be true,' she told herself. 'It can't. Edmund wouldn't do that to her. All he had to do was divorce her. Why kill her?'

A knock at the door, followed by Doyle enquiring, "You okay, Chrissie?" brought her back to her senses.

"Yes… I'll be there in a minute."

A few minutes later, Chrissie returned to the lounge, apologising for her leaving.

"Don't worry, Chrissie. I did warn you - Edmund wasn't all he made himself out to be," said Mac. Chrissie nodded her head.

"So, Mac, are we safe to return to the city?" asked Doyle.

"Yes, no reason why not. Jo Jo is in jail and he's singing like a canary. However, knowing him he'll probably get off, making sure one of his guys takes the fall for him. Either way, I've put the frighteners on him. And probably made a worse enemy as well. But hey, that's the job."

Doyle nodded his head. He felt both happy and sad for his pal. The sooner Mac retired the better. He would make sure he watched Macs back as much as he could.

"Okay. Thanks, Mac. I think we should get some shut-eye. We can leave in the morning. Chrissie, get yourself off to bed, you must be drained. You'll need your sleep and strength for the next few days."

Looking at Doyle, Chrissie realised that the passion of the earlier evening was now no longer applicable. Mac's arrival had certainly put a damper on anything happening. As she said goodnight and made her way to bed, Chrissie wondered if the situation would ever arise again where she and Doyle would find themselves embracing. Somehow, she doubted it. Such a pity. Boy, could he kiss. And he had certainly been turned on; of that, she was sure.

The following morning, after cleaning up the house and leaving it as if no one had ever been there, Doyle, Chrissie, and Mac headed back to town. The journey was uneventful.

Once there, Doyle and Chrissie settled back into the brownstone. Mac decided it would help if Tommy could continue to keep a close eye on her until after the trial.

Doyle would have preferred not to have to do so, but Mac asked, so he obliged him. In reality, he didn't want a repeat of what had happened at the house just before Mac's arrival, so that night he slept on the sofa in the office. However, about 4 am he heard the soft pad of Chrissie's feet as she crossed the office floor. Doyle continued to sleep, or at least pretend to be asleep. Slowly he felt her climb into the bed alongside him. He dare not move, for fear of arousing desire on both their parts.

"I know you're not asleep, Tommy," she whispered. "And I know you want me. So, why don't you forget all about being a PI or a cop and just be a man? It might be the only chance you get."

When Tommy woke around about nine o'clock, he was alone in the bed. Getting up he headed for the bathroom. Having had a good hot shower, shave, and got dressed, Tommy ventured upstairs, following the smell of cooking bacon. Entering the spare apartment, he discovered Chrissie finishing breakfast in the kitchen. "Sit down, Tommy. Eggs and bacon okay for you?"

She behaved as if nothing had happened. Which left Doyle wondering if he had been dreaming.

Maybe he had. But whether he had or not, he sure felt good this morning. The best he'd felt for some time. If a dream could make him feel like this, how would a good woman make him feel? And the vision of one forensic medical doctor sprung to mind – Veronica Martin. Now she could certainly make him dream, he was sure!

Half an hour after breakfast was finished, Mac arrived for a debriefing before they all headed to the court. It was going to be one big day for Mac and the force, one Tommy had no intention of missing.

During the trial, Doyle sat with Chrissie, holding her hand to give her the support he knew she needed. When it was her time to enter the witness box, she was a dependent witness. Poor Jo-Jo and his guys didn't stand a chance.

Neither did her husband, Edmund. Which was the biggest surprise. As the story unfolded it turned out that Edmund had been having an affair with his secretary for about five years. Chrissie could have accepted a younger woman but this one was about 6 years older than her, so the treachery by Edmund was even more insulting to Chrissie.

The secretary was married to a guy in the army. On his last visit home, the husband had told her he was resigning his commission and they would be moving south. The wife didn't want to leave. She loved Edmund James. When the husband got killed in an ambush while serving overseas, Edmund decided he wanted to marry the widow. But to do so meant getting rid of Chrissie.

Getting divorced would have cost him five million dollars. But, getting his wife killed would only cost him half a million. Enter Jo Jo Grimondi.

He was supposed to have Chrissie killed but when Jo Jo met her, he fancied her, so decided to seduce her and have his bit of fun. That was Jo Jo's, and by association, Edmund's undoing.

The long and short of it was, that Jo Jo recorded all his telephone conversations. Something his father had always done. The difference was the old Don had hidden his records well, while Jo-Jo hadn't, which was why Mac had managed to find them so easily.

With Chrissie's testimony, the voice recordings, the confessions of the two guys arrested at the ambush, and all the other evidence Mac, with Doyle's help, had collected, it was a slam dunk score.

Jo Jo got sent down for ten years, much to the delight of his older sister, Carlotta, who could now take over control of the family business. She would see it ran properly, not illegally.

The two guys who made Edward Brown disappear were sent down for twenty years, with no parole. And, the two guys arrested at the ambush, having given evidence for the prosecution, each got 5 years in an open prison.

As for Edmund James. Well, he ended up being sent down for fifteen years on an account of the attempted murder against his wife. But in a sanatorium for the mentally insane. He was not a happy man, but having tried to claim a defence of being mentally incapacitated that he didn't know what he was doing, what else had he expected.

Unfortunately, it had all comeback and bit him in the backside. Especially when he realised that the board of directors didn't put up much of a fight when Chrissie James walked into the office the following Monday morning and told them all in no uncertain terms that she was now the new head of Edmund James Incorporated.

You see, there was one thing Edmund had forgotten. When he had been ill a few years ago he had made Chrissie his Power of Attorney, and part of that stated that if he was incapacitated due to mental illness then she, Chrissie, got full control. Fifteen years was a long time. Poor Edmund could see his wealth slowly slipping down the drain. Or would it. Only time would tell.

Leaving the court on the last day, Mac was feeling pleased. They had done the impossible. They'd managed to put Don Grimondi beyond bars.

As for Doyle, he was happy too. The job was over and Chrissie would be moving out of the brownstone tomorrow.

"Well, Tommy," smiled Chrissie. "I want to thank you for all your help. And for looking after me. Here, this is for you," and she held out an envelope, which he took.

As he opened it, he smiled, "You're welcome, Chrissie. Besides, it was all part of the job." Looking at the cheque inside the envelope, he shook his head, "This is too much."

"You deserve it. Believe me, you were worth it; every last dime of it," and she winked at him. "Perhaps, we could do it again sometime. That is if, Veronica ever lets you down," and laughing lightly she turned and walked away, waving bye.

Mac stood alongside him. "Now, that's what you call one hell of a woman, Tommy lad."

"She sure is, Mac. She sure is," and Tommy laughed.

Mac looked at his pal and wondered. 'Did he? Or didn't he?' One thing he did know, Tommy Doyle was too much of a gentleman so he would never, ever tell!

THE CLEVER FORTUNE-TELLER

Doyle had been out all night. He'd been asked by Mr. Severino, the local Italian jeweller, to keep an eye on his shop. It appeared there had recently been at least three attempts to break into the place. Doyle had obliged the old gentleman, as Mr. Severino was knocking on a few years, and his only son, Marcello, didn't appear to have any interest in taking over the business.

Marcello had moved into the city centre to live so spent little time with his father. Mr. Severino had asked his offspring to come home and help him with the shop, but Marcello, declining, had told his father there was more money to be made in the technological world these days. Doyle was beginning to think Marcello was right, having spent another night with no view of a burglar insight.

Returning to the brownstone at about 8 am, Doyle had collapsed on the bed, sleeping until the phone on the bedside cabinet rang out demanding to be answered. Reaching across the bed, Doyle picked up the receiver, almost snarling into it. "Yea, who's this?"

"My, my, and aren't we a grumpy old sod this morning, Tommy lad?" laughed his mate, Mac.

Inspector Pete (Mac) Mackintosh was in charge of the precinct where Doyle had once been stationed; that is until he'd left some four years previous. He says he resigned, but many of his colleagues still believed he had been pushed.

Doyle laughed in unison with Mac. "So would you be, Mac, if you were out all night and only got in at 8 am? What's the time?"

Mac laughed, paused to look at his watch, then replied, "One forty-five. I'm finishing early. Had enough for the day. You up for a spot of late lunch, and a beer?"

Doyle stretched and sat up in bed. Clearing his mind, he tried to work out what day it was and what, if anything he had planned. "Yea, Mac, why not. Meet you at O'Malley's in about... err... an hour?"

Mac laughed again. "Hell, Tommy, does it take you that long to get showered and dressed? At that rate by the time you get here I'll be drunk," and he laughed again.

Doyle shook his head, telling his mate he would see him in fifteen minutes and to get the food ordered as he suddenly felt hungry. Putting the phone down he climbed out of bed and hit the shower.

Exactly sixteen and a half minutes later, Doyle walked into O' Malley's, sat down, and took a long drink of the beer Mac had sat waiting on the table for him. Five minutes after that, Molly O'Malley delivered two plates of Irish Stew and Dumplings to the table. Both men picked up their cutlery and devoured the food with relish. Neither spoke until both plates were wiped clean with the fresh homemade Irish Soda Bread, Molly had brought them for dipping in the gravy.

Mac sighed with satisfaction. "Boy, can that woman cook. If she wasn't already married to Pat, I'd sweep her up myself."

Both men laughed. Molly's cooking was well known throughout the district, and many a man had said the same thing; including Doyle himself.

"So, Mac, why are you finished early? It's not like you. Getting tired of the job?" asked Doyle.

Mac sighed before speaking. "We've got a dumb case. Nothing untoward you'd think, but for some reason, we seem to have come upon a dead end."

"Tell me?"

Wondering where to start, Mac finally began explaining. "It started with some bootleg watches. A two-bit thief got stopped by a local beat cop. He was found to be carrying a bag load of watches. The cop pulled him in as he thought they looked legit. And I must admit they are some of the best quality knock-offs I've seen for some time. The guy wouldn't talk. I got the gear checked out and he was dragged off by the fraud squad. Still won't talk. Anyway, the Chief wants the case resolved. So, it's landed on guess who's desk? Yep, yours truly!"

Doyle frowned. It seemed strange the Chief would put pressure on Mac for something like knock-offs, unless… there was more to it than he was letting on?

"So, Tommy, what you working on then that's kept you out all night?"

Realising Mac wanted to change the subject, Tommy told him about Mr. Severino's suspicion that someone had been trying to break into his shop, and how he had been keeping watch.

"I suggested he upgrade the alarm system, which he's doing, so they won't get in without waking the whole damn neighbourhood up. But having spent three nights watching, not a sniff."

Mac thought for a moment. "Sounds a rum deal. How long are you doing the nights for?"

"I said I'd give him four, done three, so after tonight, if no show, then I'm done. He's agreed. Told him with the updated alarm system, which was finished today, all we can do is see what happens."

For the next hour, the pair chatted about various mundane things, had another drink, and played a round of pool, before finally deciding to leave the bar and head away to their various homes. As they left, Mac called out, "Hey, Molly darling, if you get fed-up of that old man of yours, you can always find a space with me. I love a girl who can cook," and he laughed as Pat threw the wet dishcloth, he had been wiping the bar down with, at him.

Molly, laughing, replied, "Sorry Mac, but if I do get fed-up of him, you know my heart belongs to Tommy."

Seeing Pat's face turn to look at him, Tommy quickly left the bar without looking back. Had he done so, he would have seen Molly giving Pat the biggest, sloppiest kiss he had had in a long time. As far as he was concerned that was one couple who truly loved and trusted each other.

* * * *

Three days later, the alarm at Severino's Jewellery shop went off at 2 am.

Doyle slept through both the commotion of the shop alarm and the police sirens. As such he didn't hear about the attempted break-in until he entered Marco's Mini Market the next morning to collect some beer and chips for that night's game. The guys from the precinct got together every two weeks, workload permitting, at one of their places and played poker until late. Again, workload and whether they were on duty or not determined who attended.

"Hey, Tommy, hava you hearda about-a Severino's?" asked Marco excitedly.

"No, Marco, why, what's happened?"

"Soma-one tried to brake in lasta night."

Doyle was shocked. So, Severino had been right when he'd suspected a potential break-in. Paying for his beer and chips Doyle quickly left the mini-market and headed back to the brownstone. Dumping his purchases, he climbed into his car and went straight across to Severino's.

Arriving he was pleased to see Smithy and a local beat cop standing outside. Saying hi to the guys he went inside, being greeted by Mr. Severino himself.

"I told you, Mr. Doyle, I told you that someone was trying to break in."

"You sure did, Mr. Severino. Did they get away with anything valuable?"

Shaking his head, the jeweller replied, "No. It looks like they got stopped in the middle of it all. I found these watches lying on the floor. Must have taken them from the cases and dropped them in the rush to leave. Other than that, everything is okay."

Yet again Doyle was surprised. Who the hell breaks into a jeweller and leaves empty-handed?

"Hi, Tommy." The sound of Mac's voice made Doyle turn.

"What the hell, Mac. I spent four nights watching. I didn't see a soul. How the hell, did they know when to hit the place?" Tommy asked.

Mac shrugged his shoulders. He knew how good Tommy was at surveillance, so knew it would have to take a very clever thief to get one over on him. And to realise that Doyle was watching the place at all. He was right this was a strange one!"

Leaving the shop, Doyle returned to his office. He planned on going through his old files and records, looking for similar incidents, or perps from the past, who could have done such a job. Yet beneath it all, what worried him most, was the fact that nothing had been taken. A few watches disturbed but that was all.

Despite his concerns, Doyle spent the next couple of hours searching through his past cases, but to no avail. Finally, as the clock on the local church announced six o'clock, he went upstairs to prepare for the poker night. They would have a lot to talk about tonight. And they did.

The following day, Doyle was up bright and early. He decided to visit Mr. Severino as he needed to ask some questions, although he wasn't quite sure what, as yet. There was something about him finding the watches on the floor that bugged him. He wasn't sure why.

Entering the shop, he was just in time to watch Mr. Severino displaying a couple of watches to a customer. "This is a Rolex Submariner. The cost is 195 dollars but I can do you a deal at 175. What do you think?"

"Mmm… it seems a very nice watch. Maybe, a bit chunky for daily wear, though. Is it used?" asked the customer.

Shock spread across Mr. Severino's face as he declared, "No. The watch is brand new, as you can see from the box and the paperwork. What would make you think it was used?"

"I see. Well, there's a mark on it. As if the coating has rubbed off. Look… here… near the link," and the customer pointed to a spot on the bracelet of the watch. "Anyway," he continued, "I will think about it. I think maybe it's too heavy for what I want. Thank you," and the man quickly left.

Mr. Severino stared first at the customer, then at the watch, before returning to stare at the shop door. He appeared upset, so Doyle asked, "Is something wrong?"

It took the man a short while to answer. "I think I've been robbed, Mr. Doyle!" he whispered.

Doyle was shocked, for this was the last thing he had expected to hear. "What! How?"

Quickly locking the shop door, turning the open sign to closed, and pulling the blind down, Mr. Severino returned to the counter, and picking up the watch he passed it to Tommy. "Do you see anything wrong with the watch, Mr. Doyle?"

Now, Tommy knew he was no expert, but he knew a good watch when he handled one. Borrowing the magnifying eyeglass, Doyle looked at the watch closely. At first glance, everything appeared spot on. The perfect Rolex Oyster Perpetual Submariner Watch. One in a line of sports watches designed for diving, known for their water resistance, and corrosion. It was ideal for any sportsman's; if he only had the money. In reality, Doyle did, but he wasn't a sportsman so had never invested in such a watch.

As he examined the watch further small oddities seemed to jump out, smacking Doyle in the face. As the customer had pointed out, there was a mark near the bracelet link. It looked as if the coating was peeling. Even Doyle knew this was not possible on a genuine Rolex. And looking at the face, the colour of the time points seemed slightly off; not quite pure white? Even the face appeared to be a not-perfect shade of black, but that could have been due to the subdued light in the shop.

Handing the watch back, Mr. Severino, decided to check inside. Carefully he opened the back, almost dropping the watch on the floor when he realised that the workings within were not genuine Rolex parts. They were, in fact, bits from some old Military watch. The man was speechless; almost passing out from the shock.

Taking control of the situation, Doyle had Mr. Severino sit down while he rang Mac. He explained what had happened, saying he would wait until Mac arrived at the shop to take over.

In the meantime, he asked the jeweller some questions. "When you came into the shop after the robbery, did you check the watches, to ensure they were okay?"

Mr. Severino took a moment to answer. "Why, yes, Mr. Doyle. Every one of them was okay. But this watch wasn't one of those on the floor. This was still in the showcase, with the others, so I never checked them. They didn't appear to have been disturbed so I never thought to do so."

Doyle thought for a second, before saying, "I think it would help if, once the police have been, you double-check all your watch stock. Examine them all…"

"I'll do it now," and the old man jumped up.

"Err… no," said Doyle. "Wait until the police have been. There may be fingerprints on the cases, so it's better that you don't handle them more than necessary, okay."

Realising the sense of Doyle's words, the jeweller nodded his head and sat back down.

Half an hour later, Mac knocked on the locked shop door. Letting him inside, Doyle went over what had happened. It was decided that it might be better to remove all the watches and take them, Mr. Severino and Doyle to the police station. That way they could eliminate their two sets of fingerprints and allow the forensic bods' to check over all the watches. Mr. Severino was not overly happy at having his precious stock removed but acceded to the request when Doyle explained why it was necessary, and that he was going to go with him.

A couple of hours later, after Mr. Severino had been taken home in a police car, Doyle and his pal sat in Mac's office each sharing their thoughts on the latest evidence. "Do you think the thieves Dropping the watches on the floor was a blind?"

"Looks like it, Tommy. They pulled a fast one there on us, didn't they?"

"Too true, Mac, too true," and rising he continued, "Okay if I get off?"

"Sure. I'll finish up here. Catch you later at O' Malley's maybe?"

Shaking his head, Doyle said, "No, not tonight, Mac. Gonna hit the sack. Maybe do a bit of thinking, watch a bit of Columbo, catch up on some sleep. Catch you tomorrow," and turning he left the office. He waved to the other guys in the outer office, as he closed the door behind him.

Mac watched him go, wondering what Doyle was up to. He rarely went to bed early! 'Mmm…' he thought.

As it happened, in this instance, Mac was wrong as Doyle did go home but he ended up falling asleep while watching Columbo; even missing the moment when the great detective finally got his man or was it a woman this time?

* * * *

The following day, Doyle was up and out early. He intended to try to get to the bottom of the missing or, he should say, exchanged watches. He was curious as to how the thieves had managed to break into the jewellers? Especially after he had been watching the shop while the alarm was updated. Perhaps it was time to speak to Richard at the Alarm Company and see if there was any connection.

Arriving at Richard's Alarms, Doyle was surprised to find Mac there. 'What the hell has happened now,' he thought.

Spying Doyle, Mac waved at the police office preventing him from entering. "Morning, Tommy, and what brings you here?"

"I could ask you the same, Mac."

"Murder!"

"What! Whose?"

Following Mac through the cordoned area, Doyle was in time to see the ME and her team lifting the dead body of Alan Richard onto a gurney, ready for removal.

"We okay to remove him, Mac?" asked Dr. Veronica Martin, ME.

"Hang on a sec, Doc, I want Tommy to have a quick look," and stepping forward he lifted the sheet from the victim, showing the bullet hole in the man's chest. "Straight through the heart. Okay, you guys can remove him. Thanks, Doc," and he smiled at her.

Nodding her head, Veronica smiled at Doyle. "See you later, Tommy, Mac."

Despite himself, Doyle smiled back. She was one hell of a looker for an ME.

"Wow, Mac. Why would anyone take Richards out? I don't get it?"

"Me neither, Tommy. Well, that's it, can't do any more here. No one saw anything so it's back to the office for me. You coming?"

Doyle hesitated. "Think I'll stick around a bit. Maybe ask those questions you can't; get the answers you haven't. Someone must know something."

Mac smiled. If it had been anybody else but Doyle, he would have shut them down, but Tommy was the best detective he had ever worked with, always had been. He knew Doyle would get answers where others couldn't; including himself. Waving bye, Mac left, knowing anything Tommy found he would willingly share with him when the time was right. Pity Doyle had left the force; having been forced out due to a self-centred, unscrupulous fellow officer. Ahh… well, that's life.

After Mac had left, Doyle sauntered towards the secretary who was wiping her eyes, having been both shocked and upset at finding her employer dead on the floor.

"You okay to answer a couple of questions, please," asked Doyle.

Looking up, she said, "Are you a policeman? I've told them all I know about finding Ala… Mr. Richards, honestly."

Doyle smiled. "I'm sure you have. And no, I'm not a policeman as such, but I work closely with them. I look in places where… err… they can't always see. And I know you've given your statement but I want to ask you some different questions. Are you up to that?"

"I suppose so," she replied a little hesitatingly. "What would you like to know?"

Doyle smiled at her again. "Why don't we go across the road for a cup of coffee? Help you settle your nerves. Besides, you can't stay here while forensics are working. What d'ya say?"

Smiling in return, the young woman gathered her things and as she followed him out of the office, he said, "I'm Doyle, by the way. What do I call you?"

"Mary... Mary Charles. Is Doyle your first name?"

Laughing, he replied, "No, but everyone calls me that. Come on," and taking her arm he gently guided her across the street and into the small coffee shop.

Once they were settled, with their mugs of coffee in front of them, Doyle asked Mary to tell him what she knew about Alan Richards. It turned out to be quite a bit. Having relaxed, Mary soon opened up, telling Doyle all she knew about Richard's habits, his likes, dislikes, as well as the types of clubs he attended. By the time he dropped Mary off at her apartment Doyle knew more about Alan Richards than he thought possible. Some of the information quite unexpected.

Driving back to his office, Tommy decided to visit Mr. Severino as he had a couple of questions he needed to ask him. Entering the jewellery shop he found the father and son arguing.

"Why, just once in your life, can't you do something for me?" shouted the old man. All you do is take, take, take, but when I ask you to give me a small piece of your time you are too busy, telling me to… Oh, Mr. Doyle." Severino looked embarrassed and uncomfortable at being caught out yelling at his son.

"If it's inconvenient, Mr. Severino I can come back tomorrow?"

"No… no, please come in? Just a small family disagreement. This is my son, Marcello. Marcello, this is Mr. Doyle – he's a private investigator."

"A what? What the hell did you involve someone like him for. Hell, papa, have you gone crazy or what," yelled Marcello.

Both Doyle and Mr. Severino were shocked by the son's reaction, although only the father reacted. "Marcello, you will apologise. Mr. Doyle helped me because, unlike my son, he has a sense of duty when it comes to taking care of those in need of help."

"Go to hell," shouted the son, and quickly leaving the shop he slammed the door harshly behind him.

Mr. Severino had turned pale at his son's reaction. "I'm… I'm… sorry Mr. Doyle. You wouldn't think he was once a polite boy. It's working in the city that's made him change."

"Don't worry, Mr. Severino, I'm used to reactions like that. Come, sit down, you look a little shaken." And Tommy helped the jeweller into a chair, before nipping into the back to fetch a glass of water.

Once the old man had calmed Doyle asked his questions. He also asked him how and why he had chosen Richard's Alarms for the security update. Fortunately, the answers proved informative, meaning he would have a fair bit to tell Mac when he next saw him.

Later that evening, as Doyle and Mac sat in O'Malley's having a drink and a bite to eat, Tommy told Mac all he had learnt.

"You've got to be kidding me?" said Mac. "Really? Both Richards and Severino are members of the same club?"

Tommy nodded his head. "The very same one. Both are widowed and both wanted to connect with their dearly departed. The club is called Find Your Past Love. It's run by a fortune teller named Roman Alamina, a Russian Gypsy – well supposedly so. I believe he is more involved with the Russian Mafia than in being a gypsy," explained Tommy. "What about the watches from Severino's? Any updates?"

Mac laughed. "Oh, yea, Tommy, I'm thinking about arresting you for handling bootleg goods... ha ha ha." Tommy laughed along, seeing as how Mac was making the atmosphere light. "Seriously,

Tommy, the watch you touched, plus all the others are counterfeit. The ones dropped on the floor were the real deal."

"How much we talking?"

"Mr. Severino thinks roughly 12,000 dollars. If they hadn't been disturbed by the alarm going off, well we reckon it could have been somewhere in the region of 50,000 dollars. They chose high-end stuff. Rolex watches ain't cheap, and Severino's is one of the top stockists in the area."

Doyle whistled. That was no small amount. The question was if they've done it once then they could do it again; that is if they haven't already done so?

Deciding to return to the brownstone, the pair left the bar. Back at the office, Doyle and Mac discussed what they could do to resolve the case.

Mac said, "If this Alamina guy is behind this robbery, is he also behind the murder of Richards, and... have there been other similar burglaries which we're not aware of? I think I'm going to have to do some research back at the precinct to see if there any other cases which sound familiar."

"Mmm... sounds a good idea," said Tommy. "I think I might have another chat with Mr. Severino. Perhaps there are more of his buddies in the club. If so, we could get them to double-check their stock and find out if any are faulty. Perhaps a personal visit might be better than broadcasting it out loud?"

Doyle paused. "You know, Mac, thinking about it, remember those bootleg watches, perhaps that's what they were for. Maybe, the guy might be a bit more forthcoming now a murder has been committed?"

Mac nodded his head in agreement. "Good idea, Tommy. I'll drag him back in again tomorrow and see what I can get out of him." Having agreed on the action each was to take, shortly afterward they left for their individual homes.

* * * *

The following day, Doyle, went to see Mr. Severino to discuss with him the members of his special club. It turned out there were at least five other jewellers, all watch dealers, and all known to the old man.

After finding out their names, and closing up the shop, Doyle and Severino spent the remainder of the day visiting each one. As it turned out all admitted to experiencing a break-in similar to Severino's, but were unbelieving that they could have been duped where their watches were concerned. However, each jeweller reluctantly checked their stock and were shocked, and amazed, to discover that their valuable Rolex watches were worthless.

As each incident was situated in a different area of the city the reports of the break-ins had not reached Mac's desk, so imagine his surprise when Doyle rang to let him know the outcome of his and Severino's visits.

"You trying to do me out of a job, Tommy lad?" asked Mac, laughingly, as they later sat in his office going over the individual reports. "Hell, reads like some jewellery gang is operating in the city, doesn't it?"

"Sure does, Mac. You know, for me, it all seems to lead back to this Alamina character and his club. Trouble is, with no positive proof, how the hell do we get to him?" asked Tommy.

Both guys sat mulling the problem over. Finally, Doyle said, "Mac, are you up for trying a sting?"

Mac looked at his pal, wondering what was going around that noggin of his. If there was one thing he knew about Tommy Doyle, it was that when it came to sting ops, he was your man. "Okay, what you got in mind, Tommy lad?"

Slowly, Doyle laid out a plan of action as to how they might be able to snare Alamina and his gang of watch thieves. However, they would need some help from a couple of people, especially an attractive woman. And Doyle had one such lady in mind... Dr. Veronica Martin, the forces medical examiner!

When the plan was placed in front of Veronica, she was more than willing to oblige. Although an ME, she came from good Police stock, as her father, grandfather, and her two uncles had all been on the force. Three of them had received commendations and bravery awards, meaning Veronica was no chicken when it came to volunteering.

Of course, the fact that she would also be spending the evening in Doyle's company might also have had a strong bearing on her agreeing to be involved in the assignment?

Three hours later, a clean-shaven, but moustached Doyle, wearing glasses and a suit, and accompanied by Veronica, who was dressed in an off-the-shoulder black dress, entered the Crystal-Gazer Club, situated on one of the swankier streets of the city. They were supposedly Thomas and Veronica Maguire, a married couple who would be introduced by Mr. Severino to Roman Alamina, the club's proprietor, as new to the district, and possible potential new owners of Severino's Jewellery Shop. The couple were supposedly troubled, or so Alamina was led to believe, by the loss of their only son,

Charles, who had been in a water-skiing accident abroad.

"But you mustn't mention that out loud. Mrs. Maguire believes she sees her son, and this upsets Mr. Maguire," Severino told Alamina.

The evening went normally for any club, and Doyle was beginning to think he might be wrong when Veronica was invited to attend a special meeting in a private room. After Roman explained that he was a Fortune Teller, he told Veronica he had a feeling that she was perceptive to visitors from the other world. Veronica had acted surprised, agreeing that she was, and told him how her son often visited her. Alamina played on what he thought was her weakness and enticed her to join him for a private reading. Fortunately, Doyle wasn't going to let her out of his sight, insisting he watch the proceedings. This he did.

At the end of the session, Doyle and Veronica left the club. "Did you learn anything?" she asked him.

Doyle didn't answer immediately, he was thinking. Eventually, he said, "I think I know how they got the inside information, but I need to speak to Mac and he needs to check the alarm system at

Severino's place. I also want you to re-examine Richard's body."

Surprised, she said, "If Mac approves then okay, but why, Tommy? What am I looking for?"

"Opiates," was all he said as he drove them away from the club.

Despite the shortcomings of the evening, Veronica had enjoyed being with Doyle. And if he were honest, he had enjoyed his time with her, be it a job or no. She was certainly a good-looking woman, and the dress she wore had made her appear quite desirable.

Arriving at her home, Veronica asked Doyle in for a nightcap. He had resisted, mainly because his mind was on other things. That was until she had leant forward and gently kissed him, saying, "Good-night, Tommy. I had a delightful evening. Maybe we could do this again, sometime? Perhaps, when it's not a job?" and turning she went inside, closing the door behind her.

Doyle stood for a moment, thinking. It had been a while since any woman had kissed him on the lips. Smiling, it suddenly dawned on him, that all he wanted at this moment in time was to knock on her door, take her in his arms, kiss her soundly, then take her to bed and make love to her.

Shaking his head, he whispered, "Calm down, Tommy lad, calm down. You need to remember who she is. Not a lady to be messed with. But, oh boy, she's one a man would certainly like to… phew!"

Turning he quickly left, however, had he known what Veronica was thinking he might well have changed his mind and knocked on the door after all.

As Doyle drove away, Veronica sighed. "Oh, Tommy! I'd forgotten what a real man you are," and she sighed again at the lost opportunity. That night both their night's sleep was disturbed with dreams neither had had for some years.

The following morning, Doyle felt things were back to normal. Last night's kiss from Veronica, he was sure, had been a spur-of-the-moment thing; brought on by the relief of a job done. He must make sure she never knew how close he had come to not driving away. After all, he didn't want to embarrass her. Or get ribbed by Mac, who would certainly take every opportunity to do so, especially if he thought Tommy had any feelings towards the ME.

Entering Mac's office, Doyle told him what he had found out the previous evening at the Crystal-Gazer Club. He also told him he had asked Veronica to redo the autopsy on Richards.

"Yea, she called me first thing. I've given her the go-ahead. Something about opiates, she said?"

Doyle was surprised that the ME was in so early, but said nothing about that. "That's right, Mac. I think Roman uses some form of opiate to lull his special guests into telling him their secrets. Including, their shop alarm codes."

Mac's eyebrows raised in surprise. "What! How'd you come up with that?"

"There were some drinks on the table. When Veronica went to take one she was told to choose a different one, as she wouldn't like the one she had gone for. The staff seemed to be particular about who got which drink from which side of the tray. When I tried to pick one up, I was told no, only for the special guests. I couldn't argue otherwise we would have been thrown out.

Roman obviously didn't want me observing want went on, so I said OK and chose a different glass. Now, if those on the side Veronica didn't have had opiates in them, and if they didn't start to take effect immediately, then that means, after we had been asked to leave, was maybe when Roman did his supposed fortune-telling act. And, in doing so he could manage to entice information from the subjects without them knowing it."

"Get away with you, Tommy. That sounds a bit far-fetched," said Mac puzzled.

Doyle nodded his head. "True. But, when I asked Severino about the drinks, he said, he didn't remember much about the reading. He thought he'd had too much champagne which hadn't agreed with whatever he had drunk in the private meeting. He also said he couldn't actually remember getting home that night. Woke up in his bed, still fully clothed, so thought he must have been drunk and passed out. Felt a bit rough all day but by evening he was okay."

"Mmm… sounds feasible. Okay, let's say you are right. What has that got to do with Richard's murder?"

Smiling, Doyle sat back in the chair. He was relishing the telling of his tale. "Okay, let's say Richard's, who was also a member of this club, tells Roman, under the influence of opiates that he's updating Severino's shop. He gives him the new code. However, what he doesn't tell him, because I hadn't yet suggested it, was that he's going to be putting security locks on all the cases. Those locks are coded, no keys. My idea was, if Severino was held up during the day, he could use a false code that would set the silent alarms off in the control centre, and the police would attend. Catching the criminals in the act.

Somehow, Roman knew I had been watching the place, perhaps getting the info from Severino, which is why Richards got to finish the install. Now, I didn't suggest the new additions until after I had stopped watching the place. And, as it was done during opening hours, Roman couldn't have known about it. That's why the alarm went off when they broke into the watch cabinets. No keys, so they jimmied the locks. Hey presto, central control alert, police notified."

Mac, sat back in his chair, laughing and shaking his head. "Well, I never. Master criminal is outdone by the one and only, Tommy Doyle. You sneaky, bastard," and they both laughed at the closest term of endearment Doyle would ever hear from Mac.

A few days later, the police raided the Crystal-Gaze Club. Catching Roman Alamina in the act of having drugged his special guests to get some information, he was arrested along with his gang. They were charged with multiple counts of burglary, passing boot-legged merchandise, and anything else Mac could come up with to throw at them. He wanted to ensure the whole gang went away for a very long time.

Alamina himself was also charged with the supply and administration of opiates, obtaining information by false means, and the murder of Alan Richards. When he denied any knowledge of this, Mac was delighted to show him the toxicology results which showed the victim had the same opiates in his bloodstream that Alamina had been caught administrating to his other victims.

The other downside for the Russian was that he had recorded all the special meetings, and Mac had discovered the tapes hidden in a safe in Alamina's office. It was a slam-dunk deal and Alamina was bang to rights.

* * * *

Two days later Mac walked into O'Malley's looking for Tommy, finding him sat at the bar chatting to Pat, the landlord.

Turning to greet his pal, Tommy was surprised to discover Mac was accompanied by Dr. Veronica Martin. She smiled warmly at him, as he said, "Evening, Mac, Doc. Err… want a drink?"

"Why, thank you, Tommy. G & T please." And she smiled again as she slid onto the seat next to him.

"Beer, Tommy lad, please. I thought Veronica deserved a meal out for all the help she gave us the other night... and what better place than, O' Malley's. Okay?"

Doyle was surprised but nodded yes. "Why not. You'll like the food here, Doc. Very tasty."

Veronica smiled again. "Good, I'm famished. And seeing as how I'm off duty, why don't we make it Veronica... Tommy?"

As Mac took a swig of his beer, he had a small grin on his face. The interaction between the two was quite something to see. 'Mmm...' he thought. 'So, what exactly did happen the other night while the pair were undercover? I wonder? I really do wonder?'

PROMISE OF A NEW JOB

"Mac, Mac."

Hearing his name, Inspector Peter (Mac) Mackintosh, looked up from what he was doing to see 'Curly' (Charles Denver, Desk Sergeant) standing in the entrance to his office.

"Problem, Sarg?" questioned Mac.

"Yea, Tommy's been shot," replied Curly.

"What!" shouted Mac, jumping up from his chair. "What do you mean he's been shot? When? Where?"

Curly shrugged his shoulders. "Not sure, Mac. It came in over the radio two minutes ago. He's being taken to the Samaritans; thought you ought to know straight away."

Mac was stunned. "Yea, err… thanks, Curly," and picking up his jacket, he asked, "Sam's you said?"

"Yea, Sam's. Let us know how he is, Mac?"

"Sure," shouted Mac as he ran out of the office and down the stairs.

Half an hour later, with sirens blazing and lights flashing, Mac pulled up near the entrance to the hospital.

As he approached the doorway a security man stepped forward saying, "You can't leave that there, mate."

Mac didn't speak. Flashing his ID badge, he carried on inside the hospital, not waiting for the man's reaction.

At the reception, he quickly demanded to know where Tommy Doyle was being treated, only to be told he was in theatre. The news shocked him. Now he was worried. 'Hell, how badly hurt was his friend?'

Following the direction signs, he hurried to the theatre area where he was met by Smith, one of the officers who had attended the incident. "Hey, Smithy, how is he?" asked Mac.

"Not sure, Sir? He's in theatre, but I don't think it's too bad, only a shoulder wound. He seemed to be talking ok when they took him in."

"Thanks. Can you tell me what happened?" asked Mac.

"We were called to an incident at O'Malley's Bar," Smith said. "We found Doyle lying on the floor, shot in the shoulder. Clarky stayed behind to take statements from the O'Malley's, whilst I came here. Other than that, I can't tell you much else, Inspector."

Mac nodded his head. "Okay, Smithy, I'll talk to Clark later. Did they tell you how long Tommy would be in theatre?"

"No, Sir."

"Ok," replied Mac, dissatisfied that he wouldn't learn much more for the moment.

Two hours later, Doyle was wheeled out of surgery. It was the longest two hours of Mac's life. As the trolley passed, a very groggy Doyle raised his hand in acknowledgment of his pal.

"Is he okay, Doctor?" asked Mac, flashing his ID and delaying the man from leaving the corridor.

"Yes, Inspector. He's fine. There was a gunshot wound to his shoulder. We've removed the bullet. Do you need it?" responded the Doctor.

Mac nodded his head, saying, "Yea, it's evidence.

The doctor turned to the nurse. "Make sure the Inspector gets that bullet, nurse."

"Yes, doctor," she replied, quickly disappearing into the theatre, and returning moments later with a small plastic container holding the bullet.

Taking the item from her Mac turned towards Smith, saying, "Smithy, take this to forensics, and make sure they rush it through. Tell Clark I need to speak to him. I'll see you both in my office when I get back," and with that, he turned away to follow the trolley carrying his closest friend.

Arriving at the ward, Mac was made to wait whilst the nursing staff transferred Doyle into a hospital bed. Once he was settled Mac was finally allowed to spend time with the injured man.

Looking up, Doyle smiled wanly. "I got myself into a bit of a mess, Mac," he announced.

Mac nodded his head. "You sure did. What the hell happened, Tommy?"

Doyle shook his head to clear it before answering. "Someone tried to rob O'Malley's. Guy pulled a gun and there was a struggle. Gun went off, and I got the bullet."

"Do you know who it was," asked Mac?

Doyle shook his head. "No. Not seen him before. He took off, once he saw I'd gone down."

Mac thought carefully, before asking, "If I get a sketch artist in do you think you can give us a description of the guy?"

"Sure, but tomorrow, ok. At the moment, I'm ready to sleep. Must be the effects of the anaesthetic," replied Doyle, and he yawned uncontrollably.

"No problem, Tommy. Tomorrow is fine. We'll speak to Pat first. Get some sleep. I'll come by in the morning," and turning he left the room, stopping only to ask the nurse how long Doyle would be laid up.

Returning to the precinct, Mac was immediately inundated with questions from his colleagues as to how Doyle was doing.

Once he had satisfied the guys, he called Smith and Clark into his office. After a bit of a gruelling time, he let the two officers go, accepting he had got all the information they could offer him.

His next port of call was O'Malley's bar.

Walking into the bar some half an hour later, Mac discovered the police sketch artist sitting in a corner with Pat O'Malley, taking details of the culprit's description.

Molly, entering the bar from the kitchen, immediately came towards him. "How is Tommy? Is he okay?"

Mac assured her that their mate was fine. The wound had been seen too, but he would be spending the night in the hospital to get over the small operation he had undergone. Molly was relieved; thankful that their friend was okay.

Sitting at the table, Mac asked what had happened. As it turned out Molly couldn't tell him very much. She had been down the street at the mini-market. The incident was over by the time she got back. The first she knew anything was wrong was when she heard the police and ambulance sirens. Rushing back to the bar she was just in time to see Tommy being lifted into the ambulance. Mac realised he would have to wait until Pat and the sketch artist had finished before learning more.

Ten minutes later the police sketch artist stood up. After showing the composite to Mac, who didn't recognise the guy in the drawing, the sketch artist left the bar. He would return to the precinct, have the image copied, and then send it out to the other local precincts around the area.

Sitting down in the vacant chair, Mac asked Pat O'Malley what had happened. Pat was still shaken by the incident. Shaking his head, he explained, "To be honest, Mac, it all happened so suddenly. Tommy had just finished his lunch and taken his plate into the kitchen. I was clearing and wiping the tables when this guy came in; he seemed an ordinary type of bloke. I returned to the bar, asked the guy what could I get him. When he replied the contents of the cash till I sort of froze."

Pat stopped speaking as he remembered the fear of looking down the barrel of the gun pointed at him.

Leaning over, Mac patted his arm saying, "Take it steady, Pat. In your own good time," and he waited for the barman to continue.

Finally, taking a deep breath, Pat continued, "Well, as I said I just sort of froze. Then Tommy comes out of the kitchen. He must have seen me standing still and wondered what was happening. I don't think he saw the gun as the guy had his back towards him."

Pat paused to gather his thoughts. "Anyway, Tommy sort of snuck up on the guy and made a grab for the gun. I dived over the bar towards the pair of them, and we all ended up struggling. I think Tommy was trying to wrestle the weapon of the fellow.

Suddenly a shot rang out, Tommy went down, the guy turned and ran like hell out of the bar. I was going to give chase but I had to make sure Tommy was okay.

By the time I got outside, he had disappeared. I came back, called the police and ambulance, then did what I could for poor Tommy."

Mac had sat listening in silence, not wanting to disrupt the flow of memory. Finally, he asked, "So, would you recognise this guy again if you saw him?"

"Sure would, Mac; no problem," responded Pat assuredly, all the while nodding his head up and down in agreement.

Standing, Mac said, "Okay Pat, that's great. By the way did he drop the gun," and when Pat shook his head no, Mac asked, "Did you happen to see what sort it was?"

Pat stood up. "Yea; it was a Colt but I'm not sure which model."

"Okay, no worries," responded Mac. "We'll take a look around and see if he dropped it when he ran. Which way did he go?"

They both went outside so Pat could point up the street showing which way the gunman had disappeared. Then saying bye, Mac left, returning to the precinct to see if he could discover anything further. Maybe the officers who had been taking statements had come up with some evidence or clues, but he doubted it.

* * * *

The following morning Tommy was dressed and ready when Mac called to collect him. He was relieved as, despite the advice of the doctor, he wanted to get out of the hospital. He hated these places.

"Besides," he had told the doctor, "I will be better off at home in my own bed."

The doctor had reluctantly agreed, stressing that he must, under all circumstances take it easy and rest his shoulder; otherwise, the wound wouldn't heal properly.

Within moments of Mac arriving Tommy, release form and appointment card in hand, left the medical centre. Stepping outside, he breathed in the fresh morning air deeply, thinking how lucky he was to be alive.

"You okay, Tommy?"

Tommy smiled, "Sure am; just glad to be out of that place."

Mac laughed at him, "Well, in that case, how about we go to the precinct and have you look at the composite picture. Pat seemed to remember the guy quite well. Let's see what you think," and with that, they got in Mac's car and drove away.

Entering the precinct Doyle was soon surrounded by his old colleagues, wanting to know how he was feeling and how badly hurt he was.

"It's only a shoulder wound; can't get rid of me that easy," Tommy laughed. "Thanks, guys, for asking."

Leaving his friends, Tommy followed Mac into his office. Sitting down he picked up the artist's sketch of the man who had shot him, studying it for a few moments. Finally, he placed it back down on the desk. "That's the guy. Any idea who he is?"

Mac shook his head. "No, sorry, Tommy. No one seems to recognise him. We'll keep asking but there weren't that many witnesses around at the time of the shooting," and he sighed, disappointed that they were no nearer to finding the shooter.

"So, Tommy, what you gonna do now?" asked Mac.

Doyle thought for a moment before responding. "Go back to the office. Have a search through my records to see if the description fits anyone I might know, or have come across in the past. Oh, and get some sleep. That bed last night was murder on my back."

"Do you want a lift? I can get a patrol car to drop you off," asked Mac.

Tommy smiled. "Sure would, if you can spare it, Mac. I'm feeling bushed."

Having organised a patrol car to take Doyle home, Mac returned to his office where he spent the rest of the day searching through the records for similar cases, just in case there was a link somewhere.

Five hours later, having had a good nap, Doyle strolled down the street to O'Malley's bar, where he was immediately pounced upon by Molly. She quickly made him sit at a table in a corner of the diner, spending the next hour fussing over him and serving him his favourite dish of stew and dumplings.

Tommy made short work of the meal, as he'd hardly eaten all day so was feeling the effects of hunger. Once he'd finished, he made to leave for home, but Molly wouldn't let him go without one of her boys escorting him home, just to ensure he got there safely.

As he left the bar with Sean O'Malley, the youngest son in tow, Tommy had to laugh, thinking, 'What a fuss Molly was making.' He didn't blame her though, as he knew both she and Pat felt some responsibility for him having been wounded.

Back home it took him a good ten minutes to reassure Sean that it was perfectly okay for him to be left on his own for the night and that he didn't need a babysitter. Climbing into bed later that evening, he felt as if every bone and muscle in his body had been punched. Hopefully, a good night's sleep would cure him of his aches and pains.

* * * *

The following morning Tommy was up bright and early. The pain in his shoulder had reduced to a dull throbbing ache. Taking a couple of painkillers with his morning coffee he sat down in his office to study his records. Yet, despite spending three or four hours on the job he had no luck. He couldn't find any connection to the gunman.

Deciding he was hungry he put his coat on, laying it gently over his damaged shoulder, and was just on the verge of leaving the office when the phone rang.

Returning to his desk he picked up the phone to answer it but heard nothing in reply. He inquired, "Is someone there." He could hear breathing, so continued with, "I know there's someone there, so either speak or hang up."

A small cough was heard, then a man's voice. It was obvious he was shaking as it showed in his voice. "I… I wanted to say I'm… I'm sorry for shooting you. I didn't mean for the gun to go off like that. Are you alright?"

Tommy sucked in his breath, shocked by the comment, as this was certainly something he had not envisaged hearing. After a short pause, he said, "They had to take the bullet out of my shoulder, and I spent the night in the hospital. Other than that, I'm okay. Why did you do it?"

The man didn't answer immediately, but finally, he responded. "I'm so sorry, I just needed some money. My family is starving, and there are some guys after me. I was desperate. I know it's no excuse, but you don't know what it's like to see your kids going hungry. Anyway, I just wanted to say, I'm sorry."

Tommy realised the man was going to put the phone down, so he quickly asked, "Why don't you meet me, and tell me about these guys who are after you. No police, just you and me."

There was silence at the other end of the phone as the man considered Doyle's request. Finally, taking courage from Doyle not being mad at him, the man suggested a place where they could meet. It was in the open, and a very busy area, so any sign of police and the man would be able to disappear.

Leaving the office Tommy made his way down to the mini market where he picked up some groceries, and something to eat for breakfast, before making his way to the meeting at the shopping mall.

Arriving at the appointed place Tommy sat down, placing the bag of food on the bench alongside him.

He waited nearly fifteen minutes and had just about given up on the guy coming when a man in his mid-thirties sat down on the bench next to him. He realised this was the man who had shot him.

"Sorry, I'm late. I needed to be sure you wouldn't bring the police," said the man in a low voice.

Without looking at him, Tommy replied, "When I give my word, I keep it. I said no police, and I meant it." Reaching into the shopping bag he took out a sandwich and passed it over to the man, saying, "Here, eat this. You look as though you need it."

The man looked at the meat sandwich with relish, but placing it to one side, he announced, "I'll take it with me if you don't mind."

At this comment Tommy turned and looked the young man in the eyes, saying, "Eat. There's plenty more inside the bag for your family. So, tell me what made you so desperate that you would take a gun and threaten someone like the O'Malley's?"

Having torn the sandwich open the young man had quickly taken a large bite from the sandwich. Once he had swallowed the food he turned towards Tommy and began telling him about the sorry mess he now found himself in.

By the time he had finished, Tommy was feeling annoyed that a man with a young family could be made so desperate as to do what he had done.

As he finished speaking the young man bowed his head, ashamed of his actions. He waited for Doyle to pounce on him. Tommy said nothing, letting the young man; whose name he had discovered was Tony Walsh, calm down.

"Are you going to report me to the police, Mr. Doyle?" he asked tentatively, looking at Doyle from under his eyelashes.

Tommy shook his head. "You will need to speak to the police, so we can sort this mess out, but I won't press charges. And I'm sure neither will Pat O'Malley, once I've spoken to him. By the way where's your family at the moment?"

Looking Doyle in the eyes, Tony answered, "In the car waiting for me."

"Okay," responded Tommy, "First thing we do is get them somewhere safe, and feed them. You can come back to my place. Then you and I have to talk to the police. As it happens the man in charge of the case is my old partner, so don't worry about that. You'll probably end up with a slapped wrist from a judge, but we can sort that out later. For now, let's go," and with that he stood up, waiting for Tony to join him.

Leading the way to the car park, Tony pointed out where his car was parked. As they approached it a young woman got out of the passenger seat. She looked at her husband anxiously, a worried frown on her face. Holding out his hand, Tommy gently said, "Good afternoon, Mrs. Walsh, I'm Tommy Doyle."

Hesitantly, but only after looking at her husband, did Karen Walsh take hold of Doyle's hand and shake it. Then she breathed a sigh of relief, "We are so sorry, Mr. Doyle. Tony didn't mean for anyone to get hurt."

Doyle smiled. "I know. Your husband has told me everything. Here is some food for the kids. They must be starving," and her husband passed her the large brown paper carrier bag Tommy had given him.

"The shooting is serious, but I think with a bit of help from me, and a good explanation from your husband, we can get the matter resolved without much trouble. What I have told your husband, is that the first thing we have to do is to get you somewhere safe and secure. Will you trust me to help you?" and Tommy smiled at her to show his sincerity.

Casting another glance at her husband, Karen Walsh realised that something had to be done, otherwise they would continue to be in danger. Turning back to look at Tommy she smiled saying, "Yes, I will trust you."

Tommy returned her smile, feeling relief that he could help this young family. Turning towards Tony, he said, "Okay let's get over to my place. The kids will be safe there. Let's go." Tommy opened the car door and sat in the passenger seat.

Fifteen minutes later, having gone by a circuitous route in case they were being followed, Tony pulled his car into the underground car park beneath Doyle's brownstone building. This was the back entrance. Doyle only used this when driving his car, which he seldom did these days as he found walking more invigorating. Besides, it meant he got some exercise.

Settling the family into the spare apartment on the top floor, Doyle returned to his office with Tony in tow. He quickly rang Mac, asking him to meet him at O'Malley's bar. By the time he and Tony left for the bar the family upstairs were fast asleep. He had given strict instructions that they were not to leave the building or to answer the door.

Leaving by the front of the building, Tommy quickly searched the area to see if anyone was watching. The coast was clear so the pair hurried down the street to O'Malley's.

Entering the bar Pat was surprised to see the young man, who had held him up, walking in with Tommy. "Hell, Tommy, you caught the critter," announced Pat, a smile on his face.

"Not quite, Pat. Err, I need a quiet word with you, please," said Tommy and he moved to the end of the bar. Tony followed slowly, until Tommy pointed to a table in the corner, telling him to sit and wait.

In a low voice, Tommy explained to Pat what he had discovered, and what had led to the incident of the shooting. Whilst he was doing this, Molly had joined them and stood quietly listening, occasionally glancing over at Tony, who sat with his head bowed.

"Well, Tommy, is this true," asked Molly aghast. Doyle nodded his head. "Then we certainly won't be pressing charges. But, what can we do to help?"

Doyle relaxed. He hadn't been sure that Pat or Molly would agree to his suggestions. "First thing, is to let Tony apologise to you. He's deeply sorry for the trouble he's caused."

Pat looked at Doyle before answering, "If you say he's okay then I'll go along with you, but what about Mac. How's he going to react? He was very upset over you getting shot you know."

"Don't you worry about Mac? When he learns what I have to tell him he'll play along. Now, for the

198

moment, the family are staying at my place. What I would like you to do is let me know if any strangers start hanging around, or start asking questions about the shooting, okay."

Pat and Molly nodded their head in agreement and then the three of them went over to talk to Tony. Once he had sincerely apologised for trying to hold up the bar, Doyle and he returned to the brownstone.

Just before they left, Molly ran into the kitchen returning a few minutes later with a large pot of Irish stew and some dumpling mix, saying, "Here Tommy, take this for your tea. There's enough for all of you. And if you want some more you let me know, okay."

Tommy smiled at her, and leaning over he said, "You know how to look after me, Molly dear. When you get fed up of looking after Pat and the boys, you'll have to come and look after me," and he gave her a peck on the cheek, causing her to laugh lightly.

Back at the brownstone Doyle and Tony went up to see how the family was doing. Karen was up but the kids were still fast asleep. They would probably sleep right through the rest of the day unless the nice smell of Molly's cooking were to wake them.

Leaving the pot and dumpling mix with Karen, the two men went back downstairs to Doyle's office to wait for Mac, who arrived an hour later, just as they were sitting down to eat.

"Sorry I'm late, Tommy; got caught up in a shooting. Thought it might have been your guy but it was some gangland thugs. Something smells nice. Are you cooking?"

Tommy encouraged Mac to join them and waited until he had sat down before responding. "Well, it couldn't have been my guy who did the shooting today."

Mac's head shot up in surprise as he asked, "What do you mean, Tommy."

Pointing to Tony, he announced, "Because, this is my guy, and he's been with me most of the day."

The look of shock on Mac's face almost caused Tommy to laugh out loud. To save Mac asking questions, Tommy quickly continued. "Eat your food, and then the three of us will go downstairs and I'll explain everything more clearly to you."

Poor Mac wasn't quite sure where to look next. For the first time in years, Tommy had pulled a fast one on him. Curiosity was snapping at him but many years on the force had trained him to contain his impatience. Settling down he enjoyed what was some of the best of Molly's homemade cooking.

Half an hour later the three men took a mug of coffee each and retired to Doyle's office downstairs.

As they left the apartment, Tommy turned and gave Karen a look of reassurance that everything would be alright. She felt some relief but did not relax, and would wait anxiously for their return.

Sitting in the office, Tommy explained the circumstance surrounding how he had come across Tony, and the reason for the young man's behaviour.

Once Doyle had finished speaking, Mac let out a whistle. Then turning towards Tony, he said, "Why didn't you go to the police?"

Tony swallowed hard, knowing it would be difficult to get this man to understand the terror he had recently lived through. Taking a breath, he answered, "You might not believe me, but I did go to the police, and the gang found out. It seemed the officer I spoke to told them. I got a beating for it, and they said the next time they would hurt Karen or the kids. I was frightened; I didn't know what to do."

Mac looked up at Doyle. It wasn't the first time they had come across a crooked cop, but in his experience, culprits usually blamed the police for all their woes.

Looking up Mac realised that Tommy believed the young man. If he was right, then they had a major problem on their hands. Finally, he said, "You do realise that you are wanted for attempted murder; for shooting Tommy here, and for holding up a bar?"

"Yes, I know that, and I'm prepared to accept the punishment as long as my family is safe," responded Tony, a resigned look on his face that he would have to pay for his actions.

"What if we don't press charges, Mac. If both Pat and I say it was just an accident. Do you think the prosecutor's office would drop it?" asked Tommy.

Mac looked at Tommy, then at Tony, and then back again before answering, "Well, if you and Pat were to come in and withdraw your statements then there would be nothing to prosecute would there. Are you sure about this, Tommy?"

Doyle nodded his head in agreement, as Mac went on. "And is Pat of the same mind?" Again, Tommy nodded, so Mac said, "Well, then case dropped."

"Great. Thanks, Mac," said Tommy smiling. "Pat and I will sort it out tomorrow. Now we need to work out what to do next on the other matter."

"Excuse me, Mr. Doyle. Would you mind if I retired? I'm bush-whacked," asked Tony, rising from the chair.

"Sure, I'll talk to you in the morning, okay."

"Yeah sure, thanks. And thanks to you, Inspector," announced Tony as went to leave the room.

"No problem," replied Mac.

Tony stopped, and turning he said, "If there's anything I can do to help let me know. I feel much better knowing the family is safe," and he quickly left the room and bounded up the stairs to the apartment. That night would be the first time in a long while that Tony and Karen would sleep deeply, confident that they were in a safe place.

After Tony had left, Mac looked at Tommy. "Are you positive about this, Tommy lad?"

"Yea, Mac I am. The guy, the family, they deserve a break. Let's give it to them, eh!"

Laughing, Mac shook his head. "I sometimes wonder about you, Tommy Doyle. You're a big softy at heart, aren't you?" and both guys laughed at the comment. "Now," he continued, "tell me everything again."

Doyle refilled the coffee cups and sitting down began going over all that Tony had told him.

Tony and his young family had moved down from the next state following the collapse of his farm. The farm had been in the family for many years, but recent droughts had taken their toll on both the land and the family.

With finance short, Tony and Karen had decided to move. Tony had answered a job application and been offered an interview. By the time they arrived in town, the job had gone. The family was left homeless; high and dry with nowhere to go or live.

Tony had tried several places to get a job, but as things progressed, he got more desperate. Their cash was fast running out, so they had taken to living in the car to save money. It was one night as they slept, the car parked in a side alley, that they were disturbed by some gangland thugs.

Tony had done his best to get rid of the guys, having only just managed to move the car before it got damaged. It had been a frightening experience, especially for the children.

Managing to find somewhere else to park Tony had gone off to look for work, applying at the local docks, but with little success. As he walked away, he was approached by a young man offering him some work. It would be off the books, cash in hand, which suited Tony. Little did he realise what he was getting himself mixed up in.

The job had been going quite well and the amount of the first week's pay had surprised Tony. A couple of days later he was asked to do a special job. No questions asked, but he would get triple the amount he normally earned. What man wouldn't jump at the chance? He was too naive to realise who, or what, he was getting mixed up with.

The first few nights all he'd been asked to do was stand look-out. He was to stand at the corner of a building some thirty or so feet away, facing away from whatever was going on. Make sure you are deaf, he was told, and when you hear a whistle go around the corner out of sight and don't come back until you hear the whistle again or if the police turn up.

Not sure what it was about, Tony followed instructions. Hearing a whistle, he went around the corner of the building and waited. Nothing happened. Fifteen minutes later he heard the same whistle and came back around the building, got paid cash in hand, and quickly left the area. It was about a week later when he was asked to do the same thing again. And, following the instructions, he did as he was told.

After four weeks of doing the same thing, Tony casually asked what was happening. The result was a threat of being shot if he didn't keep his mouth and eyes shut. The incident frightened him, so he bought himself a second-hand gun. He didn't tell Karen about the threats as he didn't want to worry her. If the guy who threatened him came at him again then he would be prepared. Whether or not he would be able to shoot him was another thing.

Two weeks later, Tony was called upon to stand watch. When he heard the whistle, he quickly stepped around the corner of the building. The second whistle seemed to be taking forever. On every other occasion, it had sounded again within fifteen minutes of the first. Tony was curious.

He kept trying to look at his watch but with no light, he couldn't see it properly. Edging closer to the corner he held his arm out so the light on the corner of the wall shone down on it. Nearly half an hour had passed. 'Had they forgotten to whistle,' he wondered? He didn't know what to do. 'Give it another five minutes,' he thought.

Five minutes passed. It was the longest and slowest five minutes of his life. Finally, he couldn't wait any longer so slowly he started to peek around the corner of the building. What he saw shocked him to the core. He was frozen to the spot. Laid on the floor were three bodies. Stood over the three, were four guys arguing amongst themselves. All Tony could hear was someone asking, "What we gonna do with them." The rest he didn't hear as he shot back behind the building corner. He was shaking from head to toe.

'My God,' he had thought, 'what the hell have I got myself into?'

Carefully and slowly, he started to sneak another peek around the corner when he heard the whistle. He dare not move. The whistle sounded again. He had two choices; either he answered the whistle, or he ran for his life.

He had just started to walk away when a voice asked, "Hey, didn't you hear the whistle." Tony stopped and thinking quickly he pretended to zip the fly of his trousers up.

Taking a deep breath, he tried to answer calmly. "Sorry mate, you took so long I needed a pee; couldn't wait any longer."

The guy who had spoken to Tony was big. He looked at him suspiciously for just a moment before shrugging his shoulders, then indicating with a wave of his hand for him to follow. Tony didn't know what to do. Should he follow, and if he did what would he find.

"Are you coming?" asked the big guy.

"Yea. Sorry just checking the coast is still clear," responded Tony, managing to control the shaking in his voice.

Turning the corner, the area was clear. Had he imagined the dead bodies? He didn't think so. All he knew was, that the sooner he got out of here, the better. The boss held out some money and with a shaking hand Tony took it; not daring to look the guy in the face.

"You okay," asked the boss man.

Tony quickly glanced at him replying, "Yea; just got a bit cold hanging around so long. Err… thanks," and he waved the money in the air before turning away to leave.

"Same time next week," called the boss as Tony walked away, using every ounce of his willpower not to set off running. "You hear me?"

Tony waved his hand and kept on walking.

The next few nights proved to be the hardest of Tony's life. He was sure he had seen three dead bodies, but he couldn't prove it. He decided the best thing he could do was move away. Take the family and move on before he got caught up in something he couldn't handle.

Two days later the news hit the streets.

Three bodies had been found floating in the river; three young oriental girls. Death under mysterious circumstances the broadsheet had said. Tony was shocked. It had to be the same bodies he had seen on the dockside that evening. He didn't know what to do.

Finally, he decided he had to tell Karen. She was horrified. "You have to tell the police, Tony," she told him. "You just can't ignore it."

"But I'll get into trouble as well, because I was there, and did nothing," he moaned at her.

"Tony. You must tell them. I'm sure they'll understand, and will realise you didn't know what was happening," she responded.

He finally agreed although he doubted that it would be as easy as she said it would be. And he was right.

Plucking up the courage he had gone to a local police precinct and spoken with a detective who had taken some details. As he left the station, they had been waiting for him. They had roughed him over good and proper, threatening his wife and kids if he said anything else.

It was only later that he realised they couldn't kill him for if they did the police would look into his death, especially after having just visited the precinct.

Plus, there was the wife to think about. At that moment, no one knew where she was, as Tony had never mentioned where he lived, and despite the beating, he had kept quiet about her whereabouts. To be honest he couldn't have told them anyway, as Karen had kept moving around. Sleeping in the car had protected his family from immediate death.

Tony stayed away from the car for a number of days. Following his instructions, Karen had kept moving it. Each day she would park in a certain place. If Tony didn't turn up within the allotted time, then she would move on to the next meeting point.

He had always made sure he returned by a circuitous route, to be sure he wasn't being followed; eventually, he caught up with the family four days later. Karen had been petrified that she would never see her husband again.

Over the next couple of weeks, the family moved further and further away; never staying too long in one place. By the time he had recovered from the beating, they had virtually disappeared. The problem was, the money had also disappeared. Gas cost money, and with two hungry kids to feed things were getting desperate; hence the reason for the botched hold-up at O'Malley's place.

"Mmm," said Mac. "Do we know who these guys are?"

Doyle shook his head, shook his head, explaining, "From what Tony has said, I reckon it's the Russians. The names were unusual and they all had accents. If it's trafficking young girls, well that's right up their alley. What concerns me is the police being involved. A rogue cop or an organised syndicate; what do you think, Mac?"

"You could be right, Tommy. Time, I think, to do a bit of digging. Are you up to it with that shoulder of yours?" replied Mac.

Tommy grinned at his pal, "Don't you worry about me, mate. I can handle it; cheers," and he raised his coffee mug in salute. Mac responded likewise.

* * * *

Following a great deal of investigation, Mac arranged a meeting with the new Commissioner of Police, who was surprised, and angry, that there was still some corruption in his police force. Mac had left the office with the Commissioner's full backing to get to the bottom of the matter. It was the man's campaign to search out and get rid of rotten cops. And recently, there had been a number of very public prosecutions as a result of this campaign. If there was one thing the Commissioner hated above all else, it was a dirty cop.

* * * *

Three days later, Tony returned to the precinct where he had originally made the complaint about the bodies in the river, making sure he contacted the same detective that he had previously.

Unbeknown to the detective, this time Tony was wearing a wire so that Mac and Tommy could listen in to the conversation. Tommy had spent a great deal of time with Tony training him in what to say, and how to react.

Sitting in the precinct office, Tony told his story about being sure that he could recognise the guys who had killed the three girls found floating in the river. Using the excuse that he had to go check some details the detective left Tony for a short while.

Unbeknown to Mac and Tommy he had gone to make a phone call to the guys who were involved with the killings. When he returned, he continued taking the details of Tony's statement, before finally telling him that he would investigate the matter and get back to him, and asking Tony where he could get in touch with him. Tony gave him a mobile number that Mac had provided for this specific purpose. Then he left the office.

Downstairs Tommy, Mac, and a few undercover officers were waiting for Tony to leave the precinct, ready to act should they be needed. As it happened it proved to be very necessary, for within two blocks of the precinct, as Tony strolled towards Tommy's car, a black van suddenly pulled up alongside him. Two men jumped out and attempted to pull him inside the vehicle.

Fortunately, he was alert to this and as the men tried to grab him, he kicked out. The diversion of him doing this allowed Mac, and the undercover officers, to move in. Before they realised what was happening two police cars pulled up in front of the van blocking it. The bad guys were quickly overpowered, handcuffed, and put into the two police cars that had also pulled up.

Returning to their own precinct Mac and his officers spent the next couple of hours interviewing the three men they had arrested.

Of course, they denied everything. However, Mac finally wore them down, and when they finally accepted that they were going to be charged with murder they each started blaming their boss; Mikale Krosnvie, who was well known for illegal activities. At last, one of the guys confessed to where Krosnvie could be found, and a unit was quickly despatched along with four officers to arrest him.

In the meantime, Mac along with his Chief went to the precinct on the other side of town and arrested the detective who had interviewed Tony. It wasn't the nicest of jobs to accuse a fellow officer of corruption, which was why Mac's boss had gone with him.

An hour later Mac returned to the precinct with the arrested detective, charging him with several crimes, including aiding and abetting murder. Once he was told about this charge, he quickly started to admit everything; likewise blaming the Russian, Krosnvie, as being the man giving the orders.

By the time the interviews were over Mac had arrested a total of seven people, including Krosnvie, charging them all with averting the course of justice, bribery, corruption, and the trafficking of illegal immigrants, as well as murder. The charge sheet read like a dossier of crimes.

Later that day, the Commissioner visited the precinct to congratulate Mac and his team for clearing up several outstanding cases, as well as for taking a very dangerous man off the streets i.e., Krosnvie, plus his crew and, a couple of corrupt cops. The newspapers headlines would be extremely good for the police, but more so for the Commissioner.

That evening Mac sat with Tony and his family in Doyle's apartment explaining all that had happened since the arrests earlier in the day. The fact that Krosnvie had been taken off the streets was a great relief to Tony and Karen as they had lived in fear for so long, they couldn't quite believe it was all over.

"Well, you may have to testify in court," announced Mac. "But don't worry, you will be protected until it's all over."

"How long will that take, Inspector?" asked Karen.

"Shouldn't be too long; perhaps a couple of weeks or so. The Commissioner wants to get this moving fast, as the momentum at the moment is to send a message that he won't tolerate corrupt cops or trafficking."

Tommy interrupted, "Don't worry about having somewhere to stay, Karen. You can stay in the apartment for now until things get sorted. And," he continued, "I've had a word with Molly and Pat O'Malley, they say you can work in the kitchen if you would like. Plus, Tony can do some work at the local mini-market, which will give you both an income and help you get back on your feet."

"Oh," exclaimed Karen tears starting in her eyes. "How wonderful. Are you sure they don't mind after what happened?"

Tommy smiled. "No problem; Molly and Pat understand, and Marco at the mini-market is certainly looking for someone to assist him in making deliveries so, problem solved."

Delighted by the offers of work Tony and Karen retired that night feeling very happy and overjoyed by the help they had been given.

* * * *

Two months later Tony and his family moved out of Doyle's upstairs apartment; taking up residence in another local brownstone apartment a couple of blocks away.

Both had settled into their respective jobs. Molly and Karen quickly became close friends, whilst Tony had joined the mini-market staff, working closely with Marco and Carlotta. He had even suggested a few improvements to the products that Marco stocked, and as such, turnover had increased. The family was quickly accepted into the neighbourhood, and they in turn were grateful for the welcome they had received. All memories of the attempted hold-up were soon forgotten and forgiven.

The bad guys were brought to court, and following Tony's testimony, they were sent to prison for a very long time, much to the relief of everyone concerned.

Tommy was delighted that everything had worked out well for the young family. But he was also secretly pleased to have his brownstone home back to just himself. He never slept well when he knew there were other people in the building.

* * * *

Doyle's shoulder eventually repaired itself. Being incapacitated that way had sent him a message; telling him he couldn't continue doing what he did and that maybe he should look to taking up a new line of work. During this time, he seriously contemplated returning to the force but knew he was too old to do even that.

Meeting up with Mac later one evening he mentioned that he was thinking of retiring.

Shocked, Mac laughed. "You... retire! Come on, Tommy lad, it's not in you to retire. Besides, what will I do if you do that?"

Tommy looked at his friend questioningly. "What do you mean, what are you gonna do. You're not retiring yet, are you?"

Mac studied the wall for a moment, before answering. "To be honest, Tommy, I am thinking about it. Supposing I did? What would you say about us going into business together?"

Tommy was surprised by the comment, as he honestly thought Mac would never consider retirement. He loved the job too much. So why was he thinking about quitting, now?

"Seriously, Mac... why? You love the job. Hell, what would you do without it?"

Mac smiled. "The truth is Tommy. When I heard you had been shot, I started to wonder what the hell I was doing still being on the force. I've got enough money put by. Hell, I've had no one to spend it on for years, so I started thinking perhaps I should take it easy and relax a bit more. Work the hours to suit me."

Tommy shrugged. If he were honest, he couldn't blame Mac for thinking that way. Taking a swig from the bottle of beer he held, he said, "Sure, Mac. The work I do isn't that hard. And, if you fancy it you could move into the second apartment upstairs. That is if you're serious about quitting, and you really want to join up with me? Hell, why not. I'd enjoy having you on board," and he held out his hand to shake Mac's.

Seeing his mate was serious, Mac looked at the proffered hand, but before he could grip it, Tommy continued. "However, let's put our cards on the table, pal. You've got what... say less than five years to official retirement. Why not stay a bit longer and leave with a full pension. If you go now, you'll probably regret it. It's not that I wouldn't welcome you with open arms. But think it through, Mac. Don't let my little accident give you the jitters. Besides, where would I come for info when I need it, if not to my old amigo? And, you never know, by the time you do leave you could have made Chief… or better still Commissioner. Now wouldn't that be a glorious way to leave, ha ha ha"

Despite himself, Mac started to laugh. He knew deep down Tommy was right. He should stick his time out. Only another four and half years and then he would be ready to leave.

"You know, I like the sound of Chief," and he laughed again. "Mmm… not too sure about Commissioner though!! Thanks, pal. I needed the reassurance," and he gripped Tommy's hand warmly.

"You're welcome, Mac. And remember, anytime you're ready, the door is open to you," replied Tommy raising his bottle in cheers. "Mind you, the day you do I suppose I'll have to change the name on that door. How does Doyle and Mackintosh, Private Investigators sound?"

Laughing, Mac replied, "It sure sounds good to me, Tommy; it sure sounds good."

ABOUT THE AUTHOR

Ann Brady is an award-winning author of historical fiction, as well as of Children's Picture Storybooks and other genres. She is also a speaker and writer's mentor of many years standing.

Doyle's Casebook was one of Ann's first forays into the world of fiction writing after spending many successful years as a non-fiction writer for an award-winning website, magazines, national newspapers, and educational tutorials.

Currently, Ann works with MentoringWriters.co.uk as their principle mentor where she assists writers of all ages worldwide to understand, learn, and discover the joys of progressing their own writing journey towards being a successful published author.

She also works with the Kids4Kids Organisation a charity she set up some twenty years ago to alongside young people, initially through the element of sport, but these days through writing. To date Kids4Kids.org.uk has mentored several children, publishing quite a few of their manuscripts.

If you need help with your writing then you can contact Ann through any of the following websites:

www.ann-brady.co.uk

www.annbradybooks.co.uk

www.mentoringwriters.co.uk

www.kids4kids.org.uk

Ann's books can be found on Amazon, her own websites, and all good bookshops.